MURDER BY ACCIDENT

A NOVEL BY ERIK BROWN

This book is dedicated to Veronica, my best friend and love, who puts up with my many hours hunched over a computer and my more than occasional unprintable rants at its not understanding what I wish it to do.

Many thanks to Erik Hilton for his advice on drugs, my technical advisor retired detective Ralph Raucci, promotion and computer expert, Beth Robinson, editor Charlene Peters, and my good friends in the Palm Beach Writers group; Donald for his stories, plus Dona, Marcia, Jim, and Paulette for their advice and counsel.

Finally, thanks to the Town of Palm Beach for having so many great bars, restaurants, and parties that attract all these interesting people to observe and write about.

Introduction

With animals it is the nose that finds the scent of the ready female, the scent that creates the attraction, the desire.

In man it is something in the mind, in the imagination, created by a look or a smile that says, "Come take me."

The attraction reaches its extreme when that smile is combined with a memory of a past conquest, real or fantasized.

This subtle difference, the nose vs. the mind, separates man from animal, but only on the surface.

In man, it is as strong and overpowering as that of any animal, and because it is in the mind, it lingers long after the scent disappears.

In its extreme, it disregards all reason, throws away family, friends, careers — and even life itself in its pursuit.

No one better epitomized this than its author, Jim.

It had been several years since I had even heard his name, until that lunch with Frank.

CHAPTER 1

The Surprise Obit

Frank had suggested a light lunch at Grease, which, as the name implies, is not the spot for a light lunch. Its two-dozen TVs cover about every open space throughout the length of the long bar, a Sunday requirement because, unless my Boston Patriots are playing Miami, the game is not on the local stations.

By the way, the guy in charge of hiring bartenders has a great eye.

Tess, pretty as a button, and Lisa, blonde, gorgeous smile and high energy, were on that day.

Lisa had brought my hot dog and Coke plus Frank's double cheeseburger, described on the menu as "The Grease Beast, not for the faint of heart."

She smiled at the difference in the size of our offerings, handed me the Palm Beach Post, and gave me a wink, "Just in case you get through first."

While waiting for Frank to put away what looked like half a cow, I was able to entertain myself by reading a detailed story of a Palm Beach Country Club member who, unbeknown to his wife of 35 years, had spent a number of evenings at "Cheetah," an aptly named, upscale gentlemen's club. Apparently, the gentleman in question had taken a shine to one of the "waitress" and after many visits consisting of stuffing multiple twenties in her G-string, they had taken lap dancing to another level, eventually producing a child.

Far beyond the point in their long marriage, where his wife had paid attention to his "extracurricular activities," everything was running along quite smoothly until the wife came upon a receipt for a twelve-thousand dollar king-size canopied bed.

Though their home had 15 rooms, she was pretty certain she'd been in them all and didn't recall seeing the aforementioned bed. She hired an investigator who found the husband had set up an elaborate living arrangement for his dance partner and had, in fact, married her. The juicy details of the investigative report included photographs of the king-size bed (evidence) and both wives.

I had to admit: the second wife had, so to speak, a leg up on the first.

The Palm Beach Country Club was probably relieved to get Bernie Madoff off the front page.

Welcome to Palm Beach, America's richest zip code.

I had finished the article and was skimming the back page obituaries when a sadly familiar name came up.

"Something's fishy Frankie."

He took a swipe with his cloth napkin, missing only a dab of ketchup on the lower of his two chins chugged half his double Coke and gave one of those half-mouth-full laughs that comes out like a gargle.

Never sure whether he did it to pull my chain or, at age 83, his mind just drifted. I waited for him to respond, which, as usual, he didn't. Instead, he slid off the bar stool, stretched his six-foot-three frame and sat back down. "Boy, this joint puts out a real burger."

Finally, realizing from my non-response he ought to say something, he chose: "Tony, you could find a mystery in a kid's marble bag."

"No, Frankie, you want real? Look at this, Jimmy Patterson, remember? Nice guy I met in the Grill. He wanted to be a writer, got involved with that crazy woman with the great body."

He stopped, took another small bite and smiled at the memory. "Good guy, Jimmy, plus the last girlfriend was tough to forget at least the looks part. If she weighed 120 pounds, had to be at least 60 squeezed into her bathing suit top. She would walk her dog to the beach in that miniature bathing suit and cars were running into trees."

He stopped as though counting on his fingers.

"Actually your pal Jimmy had a series of crazy women, all with great bodies. What'd he die of?"

"A front bumper."

I finally had his attention.

"Got run over two nights ago in West Palm on Tamarind. Kids walking to school Monday morning found him on someone's front lawn."

I hesitated to let it sink in.

"Police figure he got hit sometime after midnight."

"Strange place to be at that time of night. Talk about the wrong side of the tracks. Tamarind runs through some pretty bad sections. What was he doing there?"

"Doesn't say. Seems like it's toward the end near the bridge and the car wash."

Frank laughed, "I love that store on the next block: Family Grocery, with the sign advertising beer, wine, soda, snacks, candy, Lotto and chicken wings."

"Frankie, I knew he was down and out, but not stupid. What would he have been doing there after midnight in an area most wouldn't walk through in mid-day?"

Frank held up his big hands like he was surrendering. "Right. Then coincidently have a car run up on the sidewalk to hit him?" He reached over. "Let me see the paper, Tony."

He started to read aloud: "His body was found on the lawn of the I. T. S. Curtains Funeral home. He carried no means of identification, but was identified by one of the police officers on the scene. The body will be held at the morgue until identified and claimed by a relative."

Frank put down the paper and scratched his chin, a sign he was thinking. "You guys were close, knew him pretty well years back. Does he have any relatives in the area?"

"I don't think down here. Definitely up in Marblehead."

I felt a sadness that he was gone, but smiled at memories that flooded back. "Yes, I knew him well. Great guy until the ghosts of his past reappeared in the form of some pretty crazy women and dragged him into the abyss of drugs and alcohol."

Frank threw two twenties on the bar and stood up. "Never mind the psychological bullshit, Harvard boy. Let's take a ride. I got a pal at the West Palm PD. It's Tuesday. Good chance he may be in. He's a retired homicide detective from New Haven who comes in a couple days a week as an advisor."

Frank is a buy-American guy. His Caddy was right in front. We drove a few hundred yards west on Clematis, took a quick right on Rosemary and stood in the large lobby of the station.

A couple words with the woman at the desk and a good looking older gentleman with graying hair and a deep tan appeared at a side door waving us in.

"My God Frank, how come the rest of us age and you stay the same?"

Throwing himself into a metal chair, Frank laughed, "It's easy, I was old when we met twenty years ago, and nothing's changed. I'm still old."

He nodded toward me. "Ralph, this is Tony Tauck. He's a private investigator from Boston's North End — a good Italian boy. He worked for me when I was in the insurance-selling business a hundred years ago. Harvard boy. Played quarterback. Imagine, me teaching anything to a kid from Harvard."

Ralph smiled, "Surprised they now let us Italians into Harvard. When I was a kid we certainly couldn't join their country clubs."

Frank leaned forward in his chair and dropped his voice. "What do you know about an accident down on Tamarind? Two nights ago Jim Patterson — he's an old friend that fell on hard times and…"

Ralph was shaking his head and waving his hands as if to push the words away. Silent for a moment, he looked down, shuffled a few papers on his desk, and then finally replied: "Sorry, can't help you fellows with that one. Accidents are not my jurisdiction."

I started to say, "Palm Beach Post isn't specific, but no driver in the car reported it. Isn't that a hit and…"

Frank stood up and grabbed my arm. "Tony, you heard the man. Not his area."

Ralph walked us to the door. "Nice meeting you Tony. And Frank, don't be a stranger."

Frank pulled quickly away from the curb, and then, ignoring the usual right toward the Flagler Bridge into Palm Beach, he continued straight north on Rosemary. We passed vacant lots and a couple half empty parking garages — all remnants of the failed real estate boom. Next came small single-family homes, some vacant with signs that read "Prohibida el Paso."

As Frank drove, I thought about Jim. After a few drinks, the guys were having one of those crazy arguments about what they would like to find on a desert island. As the question was passed around, answers varied: a dozen hot women, the usual food and water, and then to Jim, who, having just finished a piece of roast beef, replied "dental floss." Easy for him to say, seemed like he'd already had all the hot women we knew.

A quick left on 10th and there we were, staring at the well-groomed (other than a few feet of tire marks) front lawn of the I.T.S. Curtains Funeral home.

Frank got out first and pointed to the sign on the lawn of the funeral home. "Someone had a strange sense of humor."

He walked across the center strip and stood on the edge of the lawn. "Look at the width of those marks. That's a racing tire. Whoever hit him was driving something expensive."

I nodded in agreement, but was still bothered by the brush off at the station.

"OK Frankie, it's an expensive car with racing wheels, but what's the deal? This car, coming from the opposite side of the street, crossed the center strip, up over the sidewalk and onto the lawn, where it accidently hits poor Jimmy. Then it backs up and takes off. No mud on the sidewalk where they backed off the lawn. Someone even rinsed it down after the accident. Your friend Ralph, the homicide Dick, is aware of all this but shuts up like a clam."

"Ralph is as straight as they come. There may be things going on that they don't want to let out yet."

I yelled after Frank, who had now crossed the lawn and was knocking on the door of the funeral home." Even the paper reports it like it was an accident. Are they in on it too?"

I walked over to Frank standing by the front door. He turned to me. "No answer. Someone dies on his or her front lawn and they don't notice. No wonder business is slow."

"Body's practically still warm. What about the morgue?"

Frank nodded. "Good idea," he said and headed to the car.

As I turned to go I noticed a glass case next to the door. There was a schedule listing a notice of a funeral on Thursday, with visiting hours from 4-6. I made a mental note.

As Frank drove, I thought about meeting Jimmy. I was new to the Palm Beach scene and sitting near the end of the bar at the Palm Beach Grill. Jimmy had, as he liked to describe it, been "over-served" and was trying to get the attention of an attractive woman to my left by throwing his French fries. One of the fries hit my chest and dropped to my lap.

Like the woman he tried to hit, I pretended not to notice. Instead I ordered fries and started a fry war; that is, until Caroline the bartender shot us her schoolteacher look. We smiled and shook hands, calling it a draw.

A week later Jim and I caught each other checking out the same chick at a party and realized we were compatriots in this Palm Beach merry-go-round. Soon we were sharing beers over Red Sox games at Cucina, Patriots games at Duffy's in West Palm, or Boston's in Delray, plus chasing women at parties, benefits and fundraisers; all three a daily occurrence in Palm Beach.

Though we hadn't met at that time, it turned out we had both frequented the same Marblehead bars, including Maddie's Sail Loft and Three Cod Tavern. I had summer visits with my mother's sister, who had married and settled on Front Street, which runs along the harbor. Jim had grown up in the same downtown section and had a million stories of fishermen and other town characters in this historic sailing town.

After about a ten-minute drive south on Australian, just beyond the airport, we reached the county morgue. The morgue is part of a large cement complex and houses the sheriff, the medical examiner, and a bunch of state agencies.

A very fit and extremely attractive woman, probably close to retirement age, introduced herself as Elsa Larsen and took us into a side waiting room. Soft spoken and a careful listener, she seemed a perfect fit for a job that probably entailed interaction with family and friends of accident victims.

Frank, an expert at small talk, had noticed a Norwegian pin on her lapel and told her of growing up with his Norwegian grandmother.

Elsa and Frank immediately connected. At first it seemed to no avail. She was shaking her head. "Normal procedure is for the body to stay with us for at least 48 hours so we can perform tests, verify the cause of death and so forth. This poor fellow was brought here early Monday morning, and as soon as we opened today he was claimed by a woman who identified herself as his fiancé."

"Barely 24 hours," said Frank. "Isn't that pretty unusual?"

"Yes," she nodded, and as if to emphasize the point, shrugged her shoulders, revealing an ample bust under her loose fitting dress.

"We got a fax from the State House in Tallahassee giving us the OK to release the body."

I was trying to read the form upside down and across the table in front of Elsa, and was only able to make out the cause of death: car accident.

Frank, who seemed to be straining his eyes as well, and not just on the paper, gave me a wink. "Elsa, I know you are not at liberty to reveal a lot of details, and I am not a relative, but Jim was a very close friend who was very good to me when I was going through some tough times. Is there any way you can tell us who picked up the body?"

"No, I couldn't do that," she said, shaking her head and at the same time turning the opened file to show a scribbled signature and relationship on the release form.

Trying not to act surprised, I stood up and thanked her for her time.

Frank had his arm around her shoulder and was showing a picture of his favorite granddaughter, Sophie, as she walked us to the front door where they exchanged cards.

The old dog, I thought. He's making a move on her, but I kept still.

As our car doors closed, I turned to Frank and almost in unison came "Joan Diamond!"

"Frankie, Isn't she that hottie real estate broad? You gotta be kidding. Jim was once a good looking guy, but the years, the booze and sleeping in abandoned cars have not been kind. This Diamond chick is serious old Palm Beach, and hot."

Frank was laughing. "Tony, did you see the bottom of the form, after relationship?"

"Yeah, fiancée, plus they call it an accident. Probably easier so they can investigate on their own time without a lot of media interference."

Frank raced the big Caddie engine and headed back to Clematis. "I've seen her out with different guys — very attentive — particularly to those with money.

Of course, in Palm Beach that doesn't make her the Lone Ranger."

Frank turned to me. "You guys were once real tight. What was it with him? He had some serious looking women over the years, I mean exceptional, but seems they all had problems."

I had thought about it. "Guy had a tough childhood. Parents divorced when he was maybe eight; mother was either away working or at home drinking. As the oldest he felt pressure to become the parent. Not a good fit at any age."

Frank was listening and nodding until, in spite of knowing what Frank's response would be, I continued, "seemed like Jimmy was constantly trying to fix his mother's problems by subconsciously hooking up with a continuous stream of women with similar issues."

Frank pulled over, leaned across me, and pushed open my door. "Tony, cut the bullshit. I know you went to Harvard but you majored in sports and women, not psychology. I'll talk to you tomorrow."

As he dropped me off I remembered.

"Frankie, The funeral and a service for Harriet Fisher is at Bethesda tomorrow. If you pick up anything of value, give me a jingle."

I was parked in the lot between Grease and the pizza joint. I got in and sat for a minute thinking about one of the many great stories Jimmy had gathered over twenty-five plus years in Palm Beach.

In this tale he was working at Hermés where, as he described it, "people dressed to the nines to go out shopping for more clothes to get dressed to the nines in." As his story goes, a woman came into Hermés dressed completely in burgundy suede. Her shoes, skirt, blouse, cape and hat with a large pheasant feather — all burgundy — all perfectly matched. When he carried her packages to the door, her footman and chauffeur both greeted him dressed in the same burgundy suede outfits standing next to her burgundy Rolls Royce with, you guessed it, a burgundy suede interior.

He said he thought he'd seen it all until she came back a few weeks later. This time the lady, chauffeur, footman and a second Rolls were all in hunter green suede.

As Jimmy liked to say, "Thank God those days are over. The women of today have more important things to spend their money on, like big lips, boobs and Botox. Oh, and don't forget the latest thing, Latisse." (For those amateur face fixers, this is a system to grow longer eyelashes.)

CHAPTER 2

Connecting with an Old Friend

I had just crossed the Flagler Bridge into Palm Beach and was sitting at the light on Poinciana listening to a little Sinatra, appropriately singing "witchcraft, that crazy witch craft," when I spotted her on the opposite side of the center strip in front of Cucina, a popular Italian restaurant and late night spot for the kids. Even at a half block distance it was hard to miss that easy on the eyes, "runway strut" — you know, the walk placing one foot directly in front of the other that makes the hips and everything in between move just a little bit more than normal. With models, who are often too thin, it only makes the dress flow, but with a little meat on the bone, it's magic.

We had met months back at one of the Wellington jumping shows. I had passed a booth, and curious to see what attracted this large crowd to a small booth, I stopped to watch. Instinctively selling herself before selling her handbags, her slight Spanish accent rose and fell as she described the people in the little village and these bags made with "their loving hands." I squeezed in close to get a better look. Straight brown hair with a touch of gray surrounded a deep tan and inviting smile. Visibly comfortable in her sales role, and I suspected any other, she wore four inch platforms that exaggerated her above average height and accentuated her slender shape, slender, but not so you couldn't make out all the best parts. The crowd thinned, we shared a coffee and a few laughs.

We were together constantly for several months until a death in the family took her back to Argentina, where an old lover appeared and I became history.

As I slowed to watch, that night in the pool came drifting back. I was shoulder-deep, facing the wall, her legs wrapped around my waist, arms around my neck, bobbing slowly up and down, and bathing suits floating somewhere. It's amazing how long you can hold that weightless position in a pool.

I pulled over, jumped out, and sprinted across the center strip.

Jay, the tall good-looking day manager at Cucina smiled and put out his hand. "Tony, nice to see you. Been a while. Working on anything interesting?"

I smiled at my old friend, also from South America; in fact, Brazil, glanced around the bar area and slapped him on the back and replied, "Pursuing a hot case as we speak."

Where was she? I'd swear she had gone in the front, but the bar crowd was thin with only a few in the back restaurant section. Richard, who owns the RSVP shipping store down the street and his key guy, Danny, both Sox fans from the Boston area, were at the back side of the bar watching the Sox and Yankees go at it. Richard held up a beer and waved me over. I waved back, headed quickly for the rear door, and then jogged though the alley and the parking lot to the narrow street behind Publix.

I glanced right, and then left. There she stood on the sidewalk by the Bradley house.

Now that I had caught up, I hesitated, not sure of her response.

I yelled, "Nila!"

She turned, also hesitated, and then ran toward me and into my very welcoming arms. "Tony, I have wanted to see you but was reluctant to call after all this time. Come, come see my place, I'm at the Bradley."

There is an old saying, "A stiff dick has no conscience," to which I'd add "true enough, but it sure has a memory."

As you might imagine after these many months and thoughts of that night in the pool, the "seeing" part of "seeing her place at the Bradley" wasn't on the top of my list; setting a world record for getting us both naked was.

Nila has the softest skin and is very comfortable in the nude. Some afternoons in the past we would lie together for an hour just kissing and touching before we made love. This time we got right to it, first my cuddling and touching her from behind, then, fully wet, she climbed on top and arched her back moving to where she got maximum pleasure — first slowly, then more and more quickly until finally she finished with a shrill sound of some Spanish word I once again didn't understand, then collapsed on my chest, her mouth seeking mine.

After a full five minutes during which we had slowly unstuck our bodies and moved a few inches apart, I broke the silence. "That's about the nicest 'hello' I can remember."

She giggled, "me also."

She was quiet for a minute, then began, "Tony, I am here for only a short stay. I leave tomorrow night."

"Why? What brings you, then takes you away from me so quickly?"

"I am taking possession of some real estate that belongs to my family. I meet tomorrow morning with the broker, Joan Diamond. You know her?"

My mind raced. Should I tell her? Could I trust her? I needed to talk to Frank.

"Yes I know of her. What is her connection to the property or your family?"

"None to my family, really. She's a realtor, but also co-executor of the estate of a partner of my father."

I had to ask.

"What was the nature this gentleman's death?"

"Funny you should ask that. It's not clear. My father, who tends to be suspicious, thinks he was murdered. The official cause is a heart attack."

I lay silent for a time, as though relaxing after sex, but with a thousand thoughts. "Do you know anything more about the death or how she got to be executor?"

"I don't know officially, but my father thinks his partner and this Diamond woman might have been lovers. My father only met her once, but said he didn't have a good feeling."

In spite of her comings and goings with me, I had watched Nila interact with customers and listened to her talk of her family. She had been brought up with very strong values. I decided to tell her of our suspicion, but first needed to call Frank.

I rolled off the double bed and started to step into my pants on the floor next to the bed where I had just stepped out of them.

"Nila, I think your father might be right about this Diamond woman. I need to make a call. My phone is in the car."

"Use mine."

I lied, "The number is in the phone."

Then, buttoning every other button on my shirt and slipping into shoes without socks, I headed for the door to which I now noticed was a very nice suite of rooms.

"Don't go anywhere. I'll be right back."

She sat up in bed, arched her naked body, stretched her arms behind her back and smiled.

I assumed that meant she'd still be there. I knew for sure I'd be back.

Skipping through the alleyway to avoid being delayed by my good friends at Cucina, I thought about Nila leaving, reappearing, and now getting ready to leave again. She had been the only woman to really touch my heart since Gabriella. I loved the sex, and more than that, her company. We had become best friends and lovers. She got into my heart, then left, leaving a void that allowed Gabriella back in. Now when I woke at night, Gabriella was back. In reality she was somewhere in Milan or Genoa or possibly, though beyond her sphere of influence, maybe as far south as Florence.

Gabriella, in one short week over two years ago, had turned my world upside down. But she was gone, running "the family," a position reluctantly inherited from her father.

Frank is old fashioned and believes cell phones are a semi-necessary nuisance. So, when he answered on the first ring, I was almost caught off guard.

"Tony, I was just going to call you. I spoke with a friend about this Diamond broad; gets some of her business from attending funerals."

He paused and I could see the smile in his voice. "You know, someone dies, Joan shows up to see if the family wants to sell the dearly departed's house. She attends them all dressed completely in black, plus the veil so they can't see the tears. Seems to do her homework; able to talk as though she was the corpse's best friend."

"Got another one for you Frank, I just ran into Nila. She's up here to meet with the executor of the estate with a guy who owned a piece of real estate with her father."

There was a long pause. I knew what was coming, but waited to let him have his fun.

"Golly gee Tony, the lengths you go to find who ran over your friend. Tell me, were you horizontal or vertical when you had this conversation?"

I ignored the comment, knowing a protest would only bring more. "Frankie, the executor is Joan Diamond. Nila's father thinks there might be foul play."

Risking another assault on my sex life, I continued. "I'm trying to decide how much to tell Nila. She's supposed to meet with this Diamond chick in the morning to apparently buy out the father."

"Tell her to delay it. You don't need to get into detail about Jimmy, but there's a pretty good chance this Diamond woman is going to short her father. She needs to talk with someone in the business that can look over the property. What about that woman Veronica, who works over in the Plaza by the theater Pat Flynn is trying to save? She's smart as hell, very straight, and speaks Spanish."

I hung up and headed back to Nila's suite at the Bradley. She was still in bed. I hopped up and lay next to her.

"You made your calls Anthony?"

"Yes, your dad may have been right. This Diamond woman may not be one to trust."

I went on to tell her about Jim, his fall from grace, being run over by a car, and Joan picking up the body.

"My father had met her once with his partner, Peter. She tried to get my father into a deal where he felt she had played with the profit and loss statements to make the numbers look better than it was. He told Peter to get rid of her, but it was too late; she had him in her web."

She shrugged her naked shoulders and gave me that helpless look some women are so good at. "What should I do Anthony?"

A fleeting thought passed through, but I refocused. "I think you should get a good lawyer or a sharp real estate agent — maybe both."

I pulled out my cell.

"Here's a great gal."

I wrote down the number and laid it on the bed.

"Her name is Veronica. Honest, sharp as a whip, knows the market and speaks Spanish. Call her to check out the property and the contracts before you meet Joan."

She slid off the bed and grabbed her cell from the dresser. Apparently, no answer, as she began recording, "Joan," she turned to me and winked, "something big just came up, and I might not be able to meet tomorrow. Please call me."

I smiled, gave her a quick kiss goodbye and headed home.

CHAPTER 3

Dancing with Mom

Back at my place I settled on the couch and flicked on the TV. PBS was playing Big Band music and giving away four CD's with a membership. Some old timer was singing. "Pardon me, boy, is that the Chattanooga Choo Choo? On track twenty nine..."

I thought about my mom. She'd be cooking in the big kitchen at my grandmother's house where we lived in Boston's North End. Usually the local priest or some politician, maybe an uncle and a cousin or two would be there. It didn't matter. Whenever certain songs came on, she'd grab me. Father Crowley would give me a wink, I'd shrug my shoulders and off we'd go. I'd try to lead, but tough when you're no more than waist high.

"Your father and I would dance to this all the time," she'd say and then pause. I knew what was next. "You look just like your dad, so handsome and such a great dancer." She'd hug me a little closer, then continue, "We would dance every weekend, at one of the many clubs in Boston, or at the Totem Pole out in Newton."

My dad had gone off to the Korean War and never returned. I was too young to really know my dad except through having to take his place when she wanted to dance.

My mom, God bless her, has been gone nearly three years now but seems to visit me often.

Frank, my supervisor for my ten years in the insurance business, became my surrogate father as well as my best friend and advisor. He had recommended me in my first job as an insurance fraud investigator. Mrs. Fisher, whose funeral service I was attending the next day, was my first client and real introduction to old Palm Beach at the highest levels. She had also been helpful in connecting me with Gabriella, who, when I last spoke with her had said we would one day reconnect, but added it would be too dangerous until what she described as "the proper time." I still thought of her daily but wondered if she would ever be free.

A loud pounding on the door suddenly broke my reverie.

The door swung opened and my neighbor Shirley and the property landscaper, James, almost in unison shouted, "Tony, someone was trying to steal your car."

I ran out. The passenger side door closest to the house was open, as was the glove compartment.

I slid in and started paging through the disorganized mass of business cards: a brochure from Grey Tesh Esq. on what to do if stopped by the police, miscellaneous receipts, an extra set of reading glasses, and then, on the floor, I spotted what I was looking for — the registration and title.

I picked up the papers and stepped out of the car.

James was nodding. "I thought it seemed strange someone would go in through the passenger side if they wanted to steal your car. Looks to me, Mister T, like he was just trying to find out who you are. It's possible he wanted more, but when I saw him and yelled, he didn't have time to finish whatever he was doing. He just looked back at me and split for the bushes. By the time I got there he was halfway to Greens, heading for the rectory parking lot."

James' son is on a football scholarship as a halfback at a Big Ten school, apparently very fast. I had to get in a dig. "I'm surprised you couldn't catch him."

He gave me a puzzled look, then gestured toward the bushes as though trying to explain.

I laughed, "Guess your boy got his speed from his mother."

He grinned, and then got serious. "Do you think we should report this?"

I closed the car door, walked around to the driver side, and was about to get into the car when James, who had stepped a few feet ahead of the car, waved. "Look here, Mr. T. Appears this guy was a smoker."

I reached down and sure enough found a half-finished Marlboro. I rubbed out the fire and stuck it in my jacket pocket. "What did he look like?"

"Sturdy, like he lifted weights, about five-eight, dark hair, crew cut, wearing a tee shirt and jeans. I didn't see much of his face. When he heard me yell, he ducked his head as he left the car. Should we call the police?"

"Hold off on the police for now. I have a feeling I know who it could be."

I didn't really, but no sense getting anyone else involved. I still had my pal Sergeant Perez on the force. If needed, she'd be able to check on things, but under the radar.

I thanked James and Shirley.

As soon as they left I grabbed my cell from the kitchen table and called Frank. We chatted maybe twenty minutes about what we knew about Jim, none of which was current, about Joan Diamond, whom we seemed to know very little, and finally, Nila.

I hung up and it struck me. Was someone watching Nila, and spotted me, or watching me and spotted Nila? Either way she might be in trouble.

I jumped in the car and headed west a block and a half to the Publix parking lot. If someone was watching her place the busy lot across the narrow street from her hotel was the perfect spot.

Publix, a great employee-owned chain of stores, had just re-placed the old store and now has a parking lot half the size of a football field.

I walked slowly between the cars, looking for anyone who might be watching her place.

Seeing no one, I headed in. Ignoring the clerk's yells, I headed for the stairs. Suite 202 was at the end of the hall on the left front. I banged on the door and yelled, "Nila!" I looked down to see if there was any light under the door and spotted a small cigarette ash on the carpet.

I wondered. Was it the same guy checking out my car who was at her door listening? Had he followed me back to my place?

Back in the lobby, I handed the clerk a twenty. I knew it would be better appreciated than an apology. "I was supposed to meet Ms. Francesca and was late."

He pretended to look to see if the key was there.

"Seems to be out."

Figuring the cigarette ash had also slipped him a tip, I held up another twenty. "Alone?"

He smiled at the game. "No, with a rather large man. Older. Had an accent like hers."

"Did they mention where they were going?"

"No, they seemed to know each other well, and spoke mainly Spanish."

Relieved she was OK; I thanked him and headed back across the lot to my car.

Her father probably sent an escort. Smart move.

I made a U-turn heading back to the house and thought maybe she already called Veronica. I pushed the speed dial. In that friendly accent, she answered, Helloow Antonie, where are you? I am at Café L' Europe with your friends."

CHAPTER 4

Café L' Europe

I took a right on North County. "I'm on my way. Be there in a few minutes."

My computer wizard pal, Jonathan, parked my car. Bright young guy, jack-of-all-trades, has the parking concession, helps with social network marketing on computers, buys and fixes up real estate. He was raised in France then came to New York as a teen.

"Few of your old friends are here, Mr. T."

My first thought when I enter Café L' Europe is, "I wish I had my camera." Tastefully decorated with bright lights and ribbons still up from the Easter Holiday, these are not to be outdone by the perfectly matched table settings and china. The food, by the way, is as good as it gets. .

My friend Donald, like our former pal Jim, who I chose not to mention, is also a long-term resident and full of "the good ole day stories."

He was sitting in the dining room to the right with the owner-manager Lidia. The two were going over a menu.

He looked up and waved me over. "Tony, you gotta hear this one."

I didn't want to stop, but he's such a fun guy, I had to. I gave Lidia, who happens to be an exceptionally attractive woman with a very interesting background, the required kiss on both cheeks, and then I sat, hoping it would be short.

"Tony, you have to hear this one. A woman called from Dallas with her event planner on the line. She's here a few weeks a year, but when in town comes here often. She loves to throw little dinner parties in our back room. It seems now they want the room for a small party — for her daughter's 16th birthday. I said 'fine,' and then they started the list."

His smile told me something good was coming.

"They want us to take out the chandeliers so they can put in a trapeze, have hired a trapeze artist from Cirque du Soleil to swing back and forth over the table while they are partying."

Laughing at the image, I started to stand up.

He grabbed my arm, "No Tony, that's just the start. They don't like the wall paneling, want it removed and asked me to send a piece of the pink china, which she likes. She wants to be sure it's the same shade as her daughters dress."

Still laughing at the absurd lengths people with too much money will go to spend, I stood again as he finished.

"She wondered if we could get Rod Stewart, who they know has a place here, to sing happy birthday, and Donald Trump to greet the guests at the door."

He laughed that big hearty laugh.

"I suggested Taboo."

The group was at the long table in the rear of the main dining room. I was introduced to Nila's escort, Fernando. I kissed Veronica on both cheeks and pulled a seat in between her and Fernando.

Veronica looked toward me as though to bring me up to speed. "I know the property they are discussing. Part of that Mecca Farms deal the state got stuck with. I can't figure why Joan would want it."

Nila interrupted, "My father said it was a strategic piece of land where the Scripps Research Center was supposed to be, but then the environmentalists forced Scripps to move to Jupiter, and Palm Beach County got stuck with a worthless piece of property, plus they got a hundred million in debt."

Veronica nodded, "At the time, they figured even if the Scripps deal fell through, developers would buy up the property and they'd get their money back; just didn't count on the real estate collapse."

I flashed back to our visit with the Norwegian woman at the morgue. She had told Frank that normal procedure is to hold the body 48 hours, but a fax from the State House had allowed an early release to Joan. I was starting to connect the dots, but to where? Joan has a friend at the State House; the state is working on a plan to create value for the land; Joan knows something that isn't public and wants a deal before it comes out?

I turned to Veronica, and said, "We know the state has annual interest costs and is under pressure to sell. If a deal were in the works, wouldn't it increase the value of this property?"

She smiled and turned to Nila.

"Like a thousand per cent. Do you have the appraisers estimate?"

She passed it to Veronica, who scanned it, looking for the appraiser's signature.

She was shaking her head. "There is definitely something shaky in the works if this so called, estimator is involved. He's a former state rep, worked as a lobbyist for Steinger, the guy who set up the Mutual Benefits scam. His job was to block any legislation that affected Steinger's business, which consisted of buying up policies on the elderly then reselling them as investments. To improve the value, they had a doctor on staff change the medicals so it looked like the insured's were about to die. Sold pieces of policies off promising a 13 percent guaranteed return. They scammed about a billion and a half before they got caught.

I jumped in. "I know the case. The Coast Guard picked up a Russian trawler with twelve tons of cocaine buried under a load of fish. When they traced the money back, it was being laundered through Mutual Benefits. A lot of poor people lost their life savings. Steinger put out over three million for campaign contributions and lobbyists to block any legislation. This lobbyist got about $20,000 a month plus a $100,000 addition to his home out of the deal. It also helped that his wife was the mayor of Broward County. You want a lesson in Florida politics? Google Joel Steinger."

I hesitated, to see if Veronica wanted to continue. She clearly knew more, but nodded for me to continue, which I did.

"I saw a Wall Street Journal article two years ago and, in fact, was currently exchanging emails with Carol Tonzi, a nice woman from upper state New York who was leading the group of victims in her area. As a group they had lost nearly twenty million in retirement savings when their tax guy Richard Nichols shoved their life savings into this so called guaranteed fund."

I wondered how Veronica knew so much about this case but felt that was a subject for another day. I stopped my story and pointed to the waiter standing politely to the side. "I think this patient young man would like to take our order."

While he was taking orders for drinks and appetizers, the ladies were chattering away in Spanish. There was one word I did understand: zapatos, which seemed to be finding its way into every other sentence. Each time this Spanish word for shoes was mentioned Fernando and I exchanged smiles. I was stumped by the next most frequent word, peluqueria, but nodded and smiled when he translated it as a hair salon.

As the appetizers were delivered, shared and enjoyed by all, Fernando and I spoke of more important subjects: soccer and football. Though he said this was only his second trip to the states, he spoke English rather well. I suspected it may have been him going through my car, but wasn't sure how to flush it out.

Finally, able to take a break, I excused myself, went to the bar and ordered two cigars. I came back to the table, nodded to Fernando and pointed to the door. Once outside, I offered him a cigar.

"No thank you, I never was a smoker," he replied. Assuming he was telling the truth about smoking, I decided to tell him without detail about visiting with Nila, and then returning. He seemed clearly concerned but smiled at the ash by her door.

"She sneaks a smoke," he chuckled. "Give me your cell number. Let's keep in touch. But we need to get back; the girls will talk forever."

They were all getting up from the table as we returned. The women hugged everyone goodbye. Veronica made plans to have breakfast with Nila the next day at Cucina while I slipped out, waved to Donald and Lidia and called Frank to relay the result.

His final comment was, "Tell Nila's friend Fernando to keep her close. There's more here than your pal Jimmy getting clipped on the funeral home lawn."

As I was getting into the car, Veronica came up to me. "Tony, I know Joan Diamond — not well, but enough to know where she looks for her leads." She hesitated and smiled. "She attends a lot of funerals, perhaps thinking the deceased's family wants to sell the home."

She shrugged her shoulders and held her palms together under her chin as if in prayer. "Or maybe it's something else."

Back at my place, still thinking about Jimmy, I pulled out an old folder I had with notes and poems I had collected from him over the years. I spotted a poem written as tongue-in-cheek but somehow prophetic.

Ode to a beautiful woman and a bum

Perhaps some nights when I have left
you must be thinking, am I deft?
I take him to a party great
He only remembers what he ate
Back home I'd like to sit and chat
bout books and movies this and that
While Mr. Crude can only think
Bout getting me against the sink
I calmly smile, sit, sip merlot
He's only thinking when we'll go
Up to my bed where he can grope
While patiently I only hope
The drunken bum will sleep or go
Cause there's one thing I aught know
He seemed so nice when we first met
But first impressions cause regret
A horny bum is all he be
And don't deserve a gal like me

A horny boy indeed, but it perhaps cost him his life.

CHAPTER 5

A Surprise Guest
at the Funeral

The funeral service for Mrs. Fisher was at the Bethesda. As with many proper Palm Beach families, Bethesda-by-the-Sea was both her place of worship and the center of her religious social life. Bethesda was serious-old Palm Beach. The present church, a strikingly beautiful Gothic structure with mesmerizing stained glass windows replaced the original building, the first Protestant church in Southeast Florida, in 1926. Like so many Palm Beach homes, it has that large center courtyard, so when you walk inside, you are outside.

I dressed in the usual blue blazer, gray flannel slacks, tan Gucci loafers and favorite tie — a light blue and turquoise background under a gold and purple mesh in the shape of seashells. I say it's my favorite; Frank would say it might as well be my only. It had a history. I had worn the same tie to Mrs. Fisher's party when I'd first connected with Gabriella.

Perhaps that's what funerals do, bring back memories, sometimes in the form of ifs, or worse, the what ifs.

I thought of our last meeting two years ago, 35,000 feet above the Atlantic. That heated few moments, pressed together as one in that tight space. After the most intense two weeks of my life, Gabriella had left without warning, no goodbye. I had followed her, obsessed with the need to know. Had her apparent love been merely lust, while I, for the first time in years, finally felt love? Had her inherited position in her family caused our roles to be reversed? Finally, as with other reminders, I had pushed her back into my subconscious.

She was history, and I needed to get back to the present.

On the short drive down County Road I thought about my first visit to Bethesda, maybe ten years earlier. It was with Jim. He had invited me to play at Bear Lakes, a two-course complex off Village in West Palm.

As we finished up, he surprised me, "Tony, have you ever been to an AA meeting?"

I laughed. "Why, you think I got a problem?"

"No, no!" He said, "That's the place guys go to meet women."

"Jimmy, are you crazy? Why look for women with drinking problems. They're tough enough to figure out when they're sober."

He gave me that big smile and held up his palm. "Wait. Hear me out. Come to an AA meeting. They meet here at Bethesda. It's incredible, the disproportionate percentage of well built, attractive women at these meetings."

He paused again to be sure I'd focused. "Some teenage girls mature early, maybe too early. Now you got a young girl with age fifteen emotions and an age twenty body.

Who does this attract Tony?"

I nodded, "Grown up body, grown up men."

"You got it. Step fathers, older relatives, maybe just boys in the same high school but two years older. Some of these girls get taken advantage of. They get scars, bad memories, and alcohol and drugs help them escape."

He stopped when he saw me nodding. "Come to a meeting at Bethesda. See for yourself."

I had gone to a couple of meetings. He was right, in spades. There were lots of very attractive women, both in the large hall and at the following discussion groups. Some I had met before; most seemed to have gotten it together. But I stuck with my original premise. They're tough enough to figure out when they've got no issues.

Jimmy, perhaps having a subconscious attraction to woman with issues, almost as much as women with good looks, kept chasing what even he described as, "My dynamic duo: big tits, big problems."

When I stepped inside to attend Mrs. Fisher's funeral I was reminded again of life's many surprises. This wonderful lady had referred me to my many of my Palm Beach clients who, like her, were victims of a thriving Palm Beach business; doctors and lawyers on the fringe, hired by heirs to prove elderly and aging parents or grandparents incompetent so they might take control of their "hoped for" inheritance a little earlier. I smiled again when I thought of her other role, playing cupid, connecting me with an enigma called Gabriella, still in my daily thoughts. Even my romance with Nila, which ended when she returned home and dropped me for an old love, when compared to Gabriella, was treated with a shrug. Maybe I had just become hardened?

Harriet, as she insisted I call her, had passed away comfortably in her sleep a few days before her ninety-third birthday. By calling her Harriet I had risked the wrath of my poor dead mother who, should I be fortunate enough to meet her in the hereafter, would chastise me relentlessly for my lack of respect.

After the very brief ceremony, which I'm sure Mrs. Fisher had requested, the overflow crowd had proceeded to the open area between the church and the rectory. After a few handshakes and the normal comments: "What a wonderful woman" and "I so admired her," I got stuck listening to a woman who I could never picture Harriet giving the time of day to, raving about "how close Harriet and I were."

I smiled and nodded while backing away from her and the crowd into the Cluett Memorial Garden where I spotted Harold, Harriet's butler of thirty plus years. He was nodding to the guests and nursing a glass of champagne.

Soon he and I were chuckling over the number of young people in attendance, and how only Mrs. Fisher would have insisted on her favorite champagne, Veuve Clicquot, named after the Widow

Clicquot, who, like Harriet, had taken over and prospered the family business after her husband's death. Harold and I had met twenty years before when the grandchildren were trying to poison her for an early inheritance.

I glanced around the room and to my surprise, L D Stephens was standing in the garden on the opposite side of the small pond, staring at me and probably wondering, as I was when I saw him, what in the world I was doing there.

I excused myself from Harold, who now had a line of people wishing to talk with Mrs. Fisher's long time employee, and possibly closest confidant.

He greeted me warmly with a handshake and hug due an old friend and, at times, co-conspirator.

Though he'd been out of "the business" for many years and now owned and operated a top-notch golf course, rumors and whispers still swirled about his torrid past. Those with a stronger interest than I found searches of film archives to reveal a lot more of what appears to be the big guy than many in civilized society wish to see, but, strangely enough, in none of the films do we ever actually see his face. Blessed with a large brain as well as the body part aptly described by his initials L D, he had a plan. Unlike many others in sports, or, as he described his profession, show business, he understood that he had a limited time to shine. His years of "hard" work and sweat appear to have paid off. He saved, invested wisely, and retired long before his prime, which as an added benefit increased the value of his older films on which he still collected residuals.

We had met by chance on the golf course in Jupiter he had rebuilt and now co-owned and managed. He seems to have found the formula: take good care of your employees and the golf course will flourish. The course and his mainly female staff definitely fit the definition of being in good shape. Nonetheless, we assume the term, "taking care of employees," refers to none of the shenanigans of his prior life. That, of course, is only speculation on my part.

Years ago, I had been invited to play with L D by his friend, Jim Gabler, an attorney from Baltimore who wintered in Palm Beach.

Jim and I had met during the murder trial of a Baltimore pastor who had paid a hit man fifty-thousand dollars to kill a blind and homeless man he had insured with a series of life insurance policies totaling in excess of a million dollars.

Talk about amateurs. The victim's body was found in a bathroom stall in Baltimore's Leakin Park, with enough clues to easily catch the assailant. On top of that, when you make yourself the beneficiary of a policy on someone you hardly know, it doesn't take Sherlock Holmes to connect the dots.

Interestingly, the man who actually committed the murder, and his brother who set it up, went free. Only the "pastor" got life.

As somewhat an expert on life insurance crimes, Attorney Gabler, who thought the insurance companies that sold the policies on a blind and unemployed man were also culpable, had contacted me. He felt, and I agreed, the policies were issued where there was no insurable interest, and the companies should be sued for negligence. After all, he'd be alive if they hadn't issued the coverage.

Unfortunately, the insurance companies' deep pockets, political allies, plus ability to move from state to state to avoid laws they don't like, made it virtually impossible to pursue.

Gabler, a criminal lawyer with some interesting clients and contacts, had a relationship that went far back into L D's former life. Several hours of drinks and stories after golf created a bond between us, and once or twice a year we three met for golf and exchanged tales. (Believe me, his stories were a tad better.)

L D asked first.

I briefly explained my initial contact with Harriet was through Frank and how our friendship had evolved over the years, including a touch of the situation with Gabriella.

He was smiling and nodding particularly about her playing cupid.

He looked me straight in the eye and serious as dirt said, "Harriet was my Gabriella."

Sensing it must have been years ago, my thoughts of Mrs. Fisher with a porn star must have created a look on my face somewhere between disbelief and revulsion.

He held up his hand, palm first. "Slow down Tony."

Seeing my glass was empty, he gave me his widest Cheshire cat grin. "Let's get you a little more of that fine champagne. Find a place to sit out of this sun."

We settled into two easy chairs next to a short drink table in the library, where we were watched over by portraits of the past priests of this historic place.

He leaned forward in his chair and started in. "As you know, I was brought up in Baltimore; my dad was a fireman."

I nodded, knowing a little of his background already.

He leaned forward, took a sip of his Veuve Clicquot, shifted his big frame to get comfortable in the chair and continued: "It was almost 50 years ago. I was about to start my senior year in high school.

"One late night there was five-alarm fire in a rundown tenement block. The entire block, in fact the entire area was owned by slum landlords who found it a lot less expensive to pay off the inspectors than make repairs to bring buildings up to code.

"Even though my dad's truck was the first on the scene, it appeared to be too late. The street was crowded with men, women and children, half dressed, still in pajamas, kids crying, clutching a few possessions.

Because of the progress of the fire and the impression, mistaken it seemed, that all had gotten out, a decision was made that these buildings were helpless and containment was the only option."

He paused and cleared his throat before starting again. "Above all the noise and commotion, my dad heard high-pitched screams coming from a window on the third floor. Without thinking about his chances, he ran directly into the smoke and fire, charged up two flights of stairs, kicked in the door and carried a young girl to safety. He had barely hit the street when the entire building collapsed."

L D stopped for a minute, seeming to catch his breath, but more likely lost in his thoughts as he was visualizing his father at the scene. "As was typical of dad, he came home in the morning, joined the family for breakfast and never brought it up."

He paused again, clearly enjoying an opportunity to talk about his father who had passed away several years before.

"First thing I heard about it was my math teacher telling me she had seen my dad's picture in the paper, and saying how proud I must be."

I loved the story, but was waiting to see how in the world this brought him to Harriet Fisher's funeral.

He smiled, perhaps reading my eyes for what I was thinking. "In Baltimore at that time, there was a major push to improve housing conditions for the poor. Baltimore was to be a model for erasing urban blight in our major cities, nationally through a public- private partnership called the Baltimore Fight the Blight Fund."

I smiled and cut in. "And Harriet Fisher was involved in the committee."

"I'll say she was involved. She was chairwoman and the major contributor."

He paused again, enjoying the memories. "You'll believe this part because you've known her. A few days after the fire, Mrs. Fisher showed up unannounced at our front door. She'd even taken a cab over so as not to call attention to what she was doing. She introduced herself as a member of the Fight the Blight committee. Said she wanted to meet dad and thank him personally. The photos and publicity created from my dad's act of heroism had spilled over and her fund was becoming a major beneficiary.

"As we were just about to sit down to eat, she stayed for dinner. She and my folks hit it off like they'd known each other all their lives. Imagine this woman who routinely had dinner for twenty-plus guests, including senators, governors and foreign heads of state, squeezed in between me and my dad in the extra chair we brought in from the living room."

"She'd done her homework, knew everything about us including where I was applying to college."

He shook his head as though in disbelief. "She not only made sure I got into Princeton, but ultimately paid my full tuition."

He paused and on came that big grin. "For a 16 year old kid

who had never been out of Baltimore, it was magic. I thought she was the most beautiful woman in the world."

He stood up and reached into his back pocket. Fumbling for a moment in a side section of his wallet, he pulled out a photo of him and his dad. Standing between them was a young, and clearly very beautiful, Harriet Fisher.

I stood up and handed back the well-worn photo. "So you have known her all along. I have visited with her so many times and heard so many stories. I wonder why you were never mentioned?"

His chin dropped a little and for a moment he stared at the floor. Then in almost a whisper said "You know how I made my money. Take a guess."

I certainly did know how he made his money, but never the details.

Without my asking, he continued, almost wanting to get this off his chest. "You know Tony, life is a double-edged sword. The late sixties, early seventies was Vietnam, Woodstock, plenty of drugs and free love, and I was right in the middle of it. I got involved with a woman who had a friend who made films. First they were private, just for fun, made up situations. We'd meet casually in the park, and flirt a little, of course ending up in bed, which was 90 percent of the film. Simple stuff, pretty light acting, but somehow it must have worked because someone in the business saw the film and I was in business."

Noticing I was now leaning forward with interest, he held up a finger. "Tony, remember the double-edged sword. This is not really a fun business. You get naked with all these people watching, telling you what to do. Often you're with some young girl you met two minutes ago. She's probably on drugs, ran away from a stepfather that had been raping her since she was eight. She hates sex, but needs the money and you have to get it up and keep a hard-on for however long the film lasts. For a while I developed a problem with drugs and alcohol — never major, but enough to make me realize the money wasn't free or forever. The good news was, unlike a lot of the guys, I made money and kept it."

He stood up, stretched and continued. "Long Dong Silver Rides Again. One of the highest grossing porn flicks of all time. I got lucky, got a piece of every film shown. I was literally making millions a year and only twenty years old.

"But, back to the Mrs. Fisher part. I eventually dropped out of school. That was my second negative. Harriet didn't even know about the first, my being in porn films until much, much, later. When that came out it was three strikes and you're out."

You know, I never showed my face, always wore a mask, but you didn't need to see my face or my dick to know it was me."

"When's the last time you tried to contact her?"

"Never did, even after I got out and bought the golf course."

"You know L D, I'd be surprised if Mrs. Fisher just dropped you as a project and was never curious as to how you ended up. Have you met her butler Harold?

"No."

"Come with me."

Harold, aging, was still tall, slim and erect, as a butler should be. His build made it easy to take the slight bow from the waist he had perfected for greeting guests of Mrs. Fisher. He had been holding court with a group of women who were now drifting away. One was dressed in what my friend Cindy the designer refers to as Palm Beach Goth — lime green gauze top with a half circle of large baubles surrounding her neck. In a way, perfect attire for this Gothic structure.

Seeing us approach, he waved us over, shook my hand, introduced me to Palm Beach Goth, and put out his hand for L D.

"L D Stevens. Pleased to make your acquaintance," was the last I heard until a few moments later, after finally breaking away from Ms. Goth, I was able to join them. They were laughing and slapping each other on the back as though they had been friends forever, which in a way was true.

Harold, clearly recognizing the name, had pulled him aside to talk.

As the conversation progressed, it turned out that Harriet had indeed kept tabs on him, a fact that both relieved and saddened him. Nice, she was interested, and sad they had not reconnected.

I knew Harold had a sense of humor. We had often kidded about Boston vs. Miami sports. But our conversations were often within earshot of Mrs. Fisher.

It appeared I had missed a lot. The penis jokes were coming fast and furious. L D, who, I'm sure heard them all, was doubled over in laughter as much by who was telling the joke as the joke itself.

I stuck out my hand to L D, then Harold. "I've got to go, boys. Harold, you have my number. Let's have dinner at the Grill, or better yet that new joint, Table 26 in West Palm. Great place run by old Grill guys Eddie and Dave. It'll be my treat."

He gave my hand a squeeze and looked me straight in the eye as I imagined my father would have, had I known him. "Mrs. Fisher told me to look after you, hoped she'd live long enough to see you and Gabriella reconnect."

I shrugged, "Me too," turned and headed to the car.

About halfway across the lawn it connected — Joan Diamond and funerals. I turned back through the arches into the center area. At the entrance there was a guest book. Figuring everyone there had signed the book, I glanced around to see if anyone was looking, shoved it under my arm and ducked into the side room where L D and I had talked a couple of glasses of champagne ago.

Signatures say something about the individual. From the little I know about the subject, the signature only represents the face the person wants to show to the world. We need extremes like slashes showing a self-destruct type or size for self-worth. You need the actual handwriting to dig much further. It was a long shot, but if Joan had attended the service, maybe I could tear out the page and bring it to a graphologist.

I got lucky. After maybe five or six pages there she was, clear as can be, average size, slight slant, meaning in control but with a slight trace back line under half the signature. I knew the perfect penmanship and slant spoke to her being in control, which made sense, but the trace back puzzled me.

Then, a signature you couldn't miss: Emile DuPont. His bold signature and "All my love Harriet, You'll make Heaven even more heavenly," took up half a page. I had to smile. Definitely fit the larger than life Emile.

Memories of our meeting at Mrs. Fisher's party, the mid-fifties-year-old Emile suggesting he'd trade two of his twenty-five-year-old girlfriends for one Gabriella, then his engaging her date, George, long enough for us to connect. It brought back a rush of good feelings, and an idea.

The signatures were early in the book. Were they together? Had Emile finally traded a couple of his twenty year olds for a fifty? I kind of doubted it, but I hadn't seen Emile, who I'd recognize in a second, or Joan, who I only knew of from a distance. Seems they came at the same time and both left early. The odds were pretty good they'd come together. If not, Emile, a real Palm Beach native, would certainly know a lot more about her than I.

As I got into the car, I noticed my cell had a couple of messages, both from Frank.

I checked the time, just after three, and called him back. "Frankie, just left Mrs. Fisher's funeral service. I checked the guest book and guess who was there?"

I got his usual flip reply, "Haile Selassie."

"Guess again. Joan Diamond. She signed the book just before Emile DuPont."

"Have you seen DuPont lately?"

"No. Last I heard was months ago. He was traveling in South America with one of his college age girlfriends."

"Well Tony, he sure dispels that old saw about youth being wasted on the young. See if you can locate him. He knows everyone in town, must have a read on Joan."

"I'm way ahead of you Frank, on my way to the Sailfish Club as we speak."

He managed to squeak in, "There's a first," as I hung up. The Sailfish Club was founded a couple years short of a century ago by, as their charter says, "A group of salt water anglers interested in promoting a tradition in the sport." The highlight of their season is a weeklong fishing tournament in January. Along with the prominence of fishing, it is a very upscale yacht club with docks, a pool, snack bar, conference rooms, and fine dining on the lakeside of Palm Beach.

I drove the four miles north on County Road past the gated homes with long driveways running to a mansion on the water, some used a couple weeks per year as the owners fifth place, or sitting as a haven for overseas money.

I drove slowly, thinking about the nearly two years since we had met. I'd been involved in the investigation of a couple pretty basic insurance scams, women who ran a funeral parlor, insuring then killing and burying a non-person for the insurance, plus peripherally in the Mutual Benefits fiasco.

I passed the Palm Beach Country Club, originally built for those families whose religious preference or lack of proper grandparents excluded them from the Everglades. The club has a short but very interesting golf course, where I had played in the past with my friend Roy from New York, and a very fine clubhouse with first class dining. It is recently better known as the place where Bernie Madoff met many of his victims. Fortunately, the typical member could lose what most of us would consider a fortune and have plenty to spare.

I took a left on a street properly named Angler, pulled into the near-full parking lot, drove around by the water then back past the main entrance. I was close to giving up on finding a place where I wasn't blocking someone when, sure enough, there parked along on the waterside near the gangway to the float was Emile's sapphire blue Bentley. Figuring I'd leave before he did, I pulled in behind him.

I smiled to myself when I remembered his comment on the Bentley when we were driving to the Polo Club. "Probably doesn't hurt my image with the girls I date, makes me at least twenty years younger."

The women he dates will always keep Emile young, I thought.

CHAPTER 6

Gabriella Wakes and Visits a Secret Friend

Memories, once lost in the mist of the past, weighed down, dismissed by the crushing responsibility she held for so many lives, both living and dead. Memories that only lately, bit by bit, had been allowed back into her conscious.

Alone last night but for an unseen bodyguard, she sat in the sauna and then swam naked in the saltwater pool with only the stars and the distant Swiss Alps as her companions. Later, back in her suite, feeling more relaxed than she had at any time in the last two years, she had fallen into a deep sleep and dreamed of their last encounter, a meeting at 35,000 feet as unexpected as it was intense. Her recent dreams had relived in slow motion: his reaching around her to close the door, which in the confines of space unexpectedly pushed her against him, erasing her plans to talk, to explain; all thought replaced by raw emotion. Her half dream, half wake reverie of his lifting her to the small counter, the counter's edge causing her skirt to ride up, revealing her long tanned legs. All the while their torrent of passionate kisses continued as she had slid slowly off the counter, wrapped her legs around him and clung to him in a fit of uncontrolled passion, short in actual duration, forever in her memory.

Their unexpected meeting lasted but a few short moments, but had created memories that she now let back in, to be played over and over in her deepest sleep. This night's reverie seemed so real; she felt she could see him, smell him, taste him and, she thought, actually feel him inside her.

Gabriella Giacometti, International Mafia crime boss, had woken up wet.

For nearly two years, any thought of Tony had been suppressed by obligations and promises to the man she long believed was only a family friend. He had been described only as her adopted uncle, thus she never understood the depth of their closeness or the purpose of his constant teaching, guidance, and training until the confession by her mother on her deathbed that Vitorio Pagano was, in fact, her real father.

Less than a year later he had died and passed the "family business" to Gabriella.

Though she was conceived of her mother's affair with Vitorio, her mother had already been promised to her grandfather's business manager. To honor her family she had married, but with an arrangement made under pressure from Vitorio's family that it would be in name only. This provided her a level of protection as well. Being known as the daughter-in-law of the Mafia Don would have limited her ability to travel, paint, and study art, all activities she enjoyed throughout her entire life, but had been cut short three years earlier by cancer. Her father, perhaps the brightest of the three sons, had studied at University of Chicago for degrees in law and history, planning one day to teach. For many years he had little to do with the family business until his two older brothers were killed.

In her inherited position, now just over two years, she had introduced methods that earned her the respect and confidence of this mostly male organization. With this had finally come time for herself, her own thoughts, her own dreams and yes, her fantasies. With this freedom had come the luxury of an occasional free thought, a thought for her future, vs. "the family." When she did, Tony, the only man she had ever really loved, came back.

This was a new luxury for someone who supposedly had so much power but could not think or feel as a person, as an individual — only as the head of a huge apparatus, a cog on a machine that now, thanks to her, was running smoothly and profitably.

What to do? She had created the rumor that she didn't care, but this was a simple ruse to protect him. Her enemies, now weakened by a few strategic moves, were more focused on survival, but a renegade knowing of her feelings could use Tony to negotiate. The pull of her father and her family was strong. But they were all gone. Tony was alive. No, she couldn't walk away. Her father would roll over in his grave. Plus, she still had enemies — strong powerful men, ruthless men, who in some cases blamed her for their loss of power, a power that was their manhood.

She knew of his dalliances with other women, but as long as there were many she was secure. She also knew when Tony followed her on the plane, he had true feelings, and she understood the struggle men have between lust and love. Tony had somehow understood it, at least as much as a man can. She knew that in spite of knowing Tony's desire to express his love, she had unconsciously turned it sexual to distract from a serious conversation she wasn't able to have. It never would have worked. She could never have fulfilled the promises to her father and be "in love."

As a woman running a male-dominated organization, it was tough enough without people watching to see if she blushed like a schoolgirl when he appeared.

No, it would have never worked.

But would it now? She was still young. Daily workouts had kept that body she was blessed with fit. For the past two years she had stepped into a man's role. She had stopped thinking like a woman, except the rare times like last night when thoughts of Tony crept back in and ruffled her brain.

And what was it with Anthony? Why him? Many men had pursued her and she had felt some level of caring, perhaps love, but some combination of events, perhaps the strain of knowing her father was dying, that her life and obligations would change so drastically, had made her more vulnerable. Perhaps it had only started as a last fling, but somehow the sincerity of a man as strong and self assured as Tony, seeming to fall for her like a schoolboy's first romance, had enchanted her into the schoolgirl role. Whatever it was, it was there and wouldn't go away.

Gabriella showered and dressed quickly, barely glancing in the full length mirror at what men only dared describe in a whisper as her "to die for" body. She slipped on a plain, loose fitting tan dress, knocked on the door to the adjoining room for her watchful body guard, Joseph Gardino, then followed him down three flights of stairs to a third floor suite for a meeting with FBI Secret Agent, Emily Jones. Gardino, at 6 foot 5 and over 300 pounds, was a former soccer player who, it was rumored, could still outrun most men half his size. Orphaned as a child in Milan, he'd been supported and overseen from age five through his final year at Yale by his "Uncle Vitorio."

At Vitorio's death, Joseph's unquestioning loyalty had been easily transferred to his successor, Gabriella.

Her parents had wished to be buried in a small graveyard on the Landwasser River near Davos. Here, in the heart of the ski area where Vitorio, a strikingly handsome ski instructor and youngest son of a Mafia boss who controlled a large portion of Northern Italy, and her mother, an art history major studying at the famous Ernest Kirchner Museum, had first met.

Gabriella had flown into Zurich for a meeting with her Swiss banker and then taken the two-hour train ride to Davos, nestled in the Alps about halfway between Zurich and the Italian border. There she would visit the quiet cemetery where her parents had been buried — her mother three years earlier, followed by her father a year later.

The spectacular views through the mountain pass provided Gabriella with a feeling of peace and fond memories. In her youth, she and her mother had often taken the same train and skied in Davos.

Providence had arranged that the FBI would also have a permanent residence in the Wald hotel, where Gabriella stayed. The FBI was at the Wald because of its proximity to the Davos Convention Center, home of the World Economic Forum where 2,500 world leaders in business, politics and academics pay the equivalent of forty-five thousand dollars just to attend, and upwards of one-hundred thousand for private meetings. These are the top leaders in every field, people who make decisions that affect us all.

Also providential, she thought, as Joseph stepped aside so she might enter, was that it was Emily Jones who had intercepted Tony in the Paris airport but a few hours after their passionate meeting on the plane. Gabriella had never allowed herself the luxury of speculation as to what she might have done had these rivals kidnapped her lover, but Tony's later description of his near capture and the reason for Emily's help had opened her eyes to a possible solution to her late father's request: "Bring peace to the warring factions in the Italian Mafia."

Emily had known of Vitorio's desire to move toward legitimate business interests requiring more brains than brawn, and assumed, correctly, that Gabriella would follow. Emily and Gabriella had met and kept in close contact over the last two years, often in Davos, where both had reason to be.

It had been a mutually beneficial match. Gabriella with a few hundred "employees," had very intense methods for solving difficulties that went way beyond the standard FBI manual. Emily had access to files and information constantly developed and updated by nearly 35,000 FBI employees. Unlike the Russian Mafia and Putin, Emily and Gabriella had an informal understanding that had grown out of friendship and mutual trust.

Many years earlier, Gabriella's father, like the Sicilian Mafia and other branches in Italy, had moved their major operations to the United States, where the big money was found in our unquenchable desire for drugs. But in the last two decades, Vitorio had begun to change his family's direction. In the last few years alone, Internet and phone scams had multiplied by one thousand what the old methods had managed to bring in. Asking people to call an 800 number for free samples of sex chat lines, psychic readings, free horoscopes, or dating services allowed her people to pick up their phone numbers. Bribing or coercing low paid clerks to add an extra forty-dollar service charge to a million monthly phone bills can add up quickly. This and other semi- or non-violent but very rewarding enterprises had made even the most extreme hardliners in this male-dominated business, believers in both the methods and Gabriella's leadership.

The secrecy of Gabriella's meetings with Emily was of the utmost importance. After the revelation nearly thirty years before, and now in the headlines again, that members of the Boston FBI had been used by Whitey Bulger to eliminate his competition, any leaks to the press, even though the motives were so different, would have created havoc within the FBI and brought the notoriety to Gabriella she had worked so hard to avoid.

The Thomas-Mann suite with its 180 degree wrap-around deck, spacious bedroom and sitting rooms had been reconfigured to hold banks of monitor screens with over 100 videos of activities in the conference center as well as another 100 covering various places about the small tourist town of 12,000.

Emily Jones was an attractive red head, about the same age as Gabriella. Her mother, a Parisian, had met and married her father when he was a graduate student from theSstates, studying at the Sorbonne.

Emily, like Gabriella, was proficient in many languages, a necessity for running this important international post.

Though officially on opposite sides, a mutual respect and additional level of understanding existed between these two women who had achieved significant success and power in two very masculine worlds. As their friendship had grown, they had often discussed their roles as women in a man's world. It began first from a work standpoint, and then evolved into their specific relationships and experiences with men.

Because of the private nature of their work, neither had married, nor did they have other women friends who could even remotely relate to their situations.

As they entered the suite, Emily got up quickly, nodded to Joseph and hugged, then kissed Gabriella on each cheek. She ushered Gabriella away from the half dozen agents at computer monitors and into a private sitting room. Gabriella sat in her usual spot on the large couch in the center of the room facing the sliding glass doors now open to the balcony and the scenic view of the mountains beyond.

Gabriella, who was running a business where staying alive often depended on being aware of changes in people and her environment, smiled to herself when she saw Emily. She first noticed Emily's hair was a little less businesslike; her eyes seemed to hold a secret, and even her lipstick had a little more color. But then came the easy part. Her usual business suit had been replaced by a slim fitting flowered skirt and frilled light purple blouse, both of which showed off her athletic but very feminine shape.

Gabriella waited and watched.

Emily, wanting to steer the conversation to her own situation and/or perhaps noticing something different in Gabriella, spoke first. "Gabriella, I am jealous of how you can dress so simply and look so feminine."

Gabriella hesitated, and then replied, "You can tell? Do I look different? It's Tony; I had a dream about our last meeting on the plane, just before you helped him escape from my rivals."

Emily smiled a knowing smile, "You never discussed that meeting in detail, but those lavatories are pretty close quarters. There are only a couple of things two people can do in there, and I suspected you weren't washing your hands."

Gabriella laughed. "The sink definitely came into play."

Achieving her lead-in, Emily continued, "Must be in the stars. I too have become romantically involved."

Gabriella stood and hugged her friend. "I am so happy for you. Tell me everything."

CHAPTER 7

Emile at the Sailfish Club

I stopped at the reception desk. "Looks like a big crowd today, what's the event?"

"Mrs. Coudert has her Coudert Institute meeting today."

"Oh yes, I've been to some of her meetings. She manages to bring in some very important people. Very topical. What is today's subject?"

"She has speakers from the Naval War College. I looked in a moment ago; they are discussing China."

She sat back and smiled, "Mrs. Coudert is a very big supporter of women's rights, has had quite a career. She's made things better for all of us."

Then, realizing she was off subject, asked, "You are here to see?"

"I'm looking for Mr. DuPont."

"Is he expecting you?"

Knowing he wouldn't be offended, I replied, "Yes."

"I believe he's out by the pool."

In a backhanded way, Emile had helped to connect me to Gabriella. Unknown to me until much later, Emile and Gabriella's father, Vitorio Pagano, had been friends while students at the University of Chicago. Deaths of two older brothers had resulted in Vitorio taking over the "family" business. Emile, too, was called back out of academia when his family's Palm Beach law firm needed him as well.

Vitorio became an off-the-record client of his friend Emile.

I walked slowly down a hallway admiring the old black and white photos of club members and guests standing with their giant sailfish trophies. I noticed the name under one of them: Gerald Diamond — a relative or coincidence?

Emile, whose long slim frame almost fit in the lounge chair with just his feet draped off the end, put down his book and jumped up when he saw me.

"Tony, so nice to see you. The desk called and said you were here." He slapped me on the back and reached out to shake hands, then grabbed my arm and led me to the bar.

"Here, let's sit in the shade. Tell me all about yourself. What gorgeous woman are you currently dating? Ever hear from that magnificent Italian woman? My God she was exquisite."

Same old Emile — always women, always fun — an interesting combination for the managing partner in the town's most prestigious law firm.

"I was flipping through the book at Mrs. Fisher's funeral to see if there were people I knew, and noticed you signed in, but didn't see you in the courtyard after the service. You didn't stay?"

"No Tony, I was with a client. We didn't stay for the champagne. We had to get back to my office for a quick look at some papers."

Still digging, I replied, "An attractive young woman I hope."

"Attractive and a woman, but not as young as I like, but just as well; I try to separate business and pleasure."

Getting nowhere and knowing he was too smart to try and game, I decided on the direct approach. "Is your client Joan Diamond? I see she signed the book just in front of you?"

"Because we are friends, Tony, I know you will respect my confiding in you, I will say yes, but sorry I can't go further than that."

"I appreciate that Emile. Actually, I was going to ask you about Joan Diamond regarding another general matter, but I'll pass."

He frowned, causing the mole on his upper lip to drop. He was quiet for a moment. "Tony, you are looking for general information on Joan, who is a native of Palm Beach, and you need to talk to another native. I can do that with no conflict."

He turned and spoke to the bartender. "Jay, could I get a pen and paper for my friend?"

Jay, the bartender, was tall, well built, with longish dark hair — that sort of wavy unkempt look — quite handsome. He smiled and passed the paper and pen to Emile.

"Yes sir, Mr. DuPont."

Emile scribbled out a phone number and passed it to me. I put it in my pocket without looking.

"Thanks Jay, this is my friend Tony Tauck." He winked at Jay and said, "Take care of him when he comes in. He's an old friend, and one of us."

When Jay smiled at the, "one of us," comment, I assumed they shared the same taste in women — young and good-looking.

"Anything he wants put it on my bill."

"We need to watch some polo together, Tony, or just hang out. Have you been to the new spot over in West Palm, Table 26? Eddie, Dave and some others from the Grill are the owners; it's the new hot spot. Max, the bartender, is an interesting young guy who traveled from Mexico to the southern end of the continent alone on his motorcycle. Has a new baby girl, Gabriella. Familiar name?"

He hesitated to catch my reaction.

I explained my non-situation with Gabriella. Then he explained his uncomplicated situation with women, all legal, but half his age. We shook hands, agreed to meet again, and I left.

On the way out, I passed what appeared to be a photo of Hemingway standing next to his catch, and realized I forgot to ask if the Diamond photo was a Joan relative. I'll see him again.

I wondered again what had pushed him to his current state of extreme non-commitment. Then, smiling to myself as I drove, thought, "Who am I to talk?"

As I pulled into my space, I wondered about Joan and her thing with funerals.

I was meeting my friend Sergeant Perez in the morning. Maybe she would know something more.

CHAPTER 8

Sergeant Perez at Greens

I came back from my morning workout at Ultima Fitness, where I go religiously (every once in a while). The TV was on with another pharmaceutical they're trying to push — Andro something. I must have seen the ad twenty times before I realized what it was for. I guess listening to all the side effects had curbed my interest. Plus, the last thing I need is something that increases my sex drive.

Apparently, you rub this stuff under your armpit to increase male testosterone. The enormous sized letters in the ad seem to suggest something increasing in size. They ought to sell it with a good sexy deodorant. One attracts the women; the other helps you do something about it. You just have to remember which armpit to lift at what time.

I smiled as they listed the complications, which included blood clots in the legs and swelling of the feet — I guess caused by all that extra weight in your shorts.

I clicked off the TV.

I had just enough time to take a quick shower and meet Perez. She's my pal on the Palm Beach Police. If anyone could clue me in on the Diamond woman, Perez could. Once you get past the hot frame and million-dollar smile, you get to the real goods — smart as hell with an almost photographic memory. Her reputation for straight play has given her a lot of trust in areas where most of us can't go. For a guy who plays loose with the rules (think none), I can go places or do things she can't. This makes our friendship a serious asset to both.

We had talked the night before. After going through the usual chitchat and planning where to meet, I brought up Joan.

"Tony," she had said, "I can give you a read on her by naming her two poodles: Percy and Cloey. I'll give you a little homework assignment. These names are short for Persephone and Cloisonne.

I had Googled Persephone, found that was Hades' wife, and a cloisonné, it turns out, is a decorated urn often used for cremations.

This should be an interesting breakfast.

We were meeting at Green's. It was the place of our first meeting; that is if you don't count her giving me a speeding ticket and laughing when I handed her my grandfather's Boston Police Detective badge.

My grandfather was my hero growing up, and I had wanted to join the police force like my Gramps, but having been married just out of college to a sweet, sweet woman with a mother who had come from nothing, married for money, and wanted the same for her daughter, marrying a Boston cop would have been too much to explain to her Palm Beach friends. I settled on the insurance business, which was bad enough. Sadly, that marriage couldn't survive the mother's meddling and had been over for many years.

Green's has been there since the days of Jack Kennedy's winter White House which was just a couple miles north on the same North County Road as Green's. It's across the street from the Catholic Church he attended, named Saint Edwards.

It was only a short walk from my place, but I drove over figuring I'd be heading out afterwards to meet Frank.

Kenny, the manager, was doing an antioxidant test on a woman at a table in the back.

Deborah, with the million-dollar smile, was looking on. She's a student intern, studying for her degree as a pharmacist.

It was a little early, so I headed through the beach section, which has everything but the salt water: sun-block lotions for pre-beach, salves for sunburns, plus shelves of beach toys for the kids.

My young friend, Danny, who can Google the answer to problems on his cell — in seconds compared to the hour it would take me to do on my computer — handed me the Shiny Sheet for all the local news plus photos of fundraisers and celebs.

I took a table at the street end. As usual, the bar was populated by the early morning regulars. Dr. Rose was always ready with a story or a joke. A retired dentist, he is now a nationally recognized sculptor. Fay, retired from the county, now writes novels and parties with his wife Nancy, the quick-witted head waitress with a wisecrack about everything and everyone. She was currently exchanging barbs with Chick, a retired painting contractor now caring for an older Palm Beach matron and her property.

I took a seat at the far end toward the street, where we could talk without whispering, and checked the day's fair in the paper.

As usual, I got my money's worth. I read an article about a Saudi Ambassador caught in an undiplomatic position with two Filipino girls, and had just started an article on another divorce and remarriage when I saw Perez come in through the back door. She was dressed in plain clothes — loose fitting but not enough to hide the goods. She gave me her usual motherly hug, though I suspect she's probably close to my age. She sat very straight in her chair, strict upbringing by a widowed mother with four girls and a strong sense of what's proper. Sonja, who honestly doesn't seem to know she's better than good looking, once told me there were no mirrors in the house; her mother knew looks are a double-edged sword and wanted to protect them from its sharper edge.

She signaled to Patti for her usual coffee in a takeout cup. "Stays hot longer," she had once explained.

When Patti brought her coffee, I kidded, "Word is Patti was quite something in her youth. She was named Broward County Brat in her high school yearbook. They say her post-graduation exploits are legendary."

Patti gave a smile that didn't confirm, but certainly didn't deny the comment.

Perez said, "Don't pay any attention to him, Patti. He's got a skeleton or two in his own closet."

Perez, seeing the paper, asked, "What's the Shiny Sheet gossip for today?"

I turned the paper so she could read the divorce article.

"Do you know her, Perez? I've seen her around at the Grill and at parties. She's got a fake Russian accent. Looks like she scored big. Isn't this guy a DuPont on his mother's side?"

She nodded. "Word is she's screwed everything in Palm Beach but the lamp post. Been his mistress for some time."

She was laughing, "You know what happens when a mistress gets married?"

"No, what?"

"Creates a job opening."

She took a sip of coffee. "What trouble are you getting into now, Anthony? You sure can pick-em. Joan Diamond. Doesn't get more complicated than that."

I laughed, and said, "I'll say. I looked up the names of her poodles. Cloisonne is a Chinese burial urn and Persephone is who Hades captured and decided to keep as his wife. What is Joan, a zombie worshipper or something?"

"You're closer than you think. I don't know her whole history, but it seems her mother was major society, and like many of the wealthy of that era, too busy to pay much attention to her children other than have the nanny dress them up for cocktail hour and parade them in for a quick hello. A nanny from Haiti who had a fascination with death and the occult raised her. Took little Joanie along as she attended funerals, sometimes several in a day. Apparently would take the child with her to kneel at the casket and speak to the dead.

Haitians are mainly Catholics, but somehow manage to mix in mild forms of Voodoo from their African heritage."

Noticing the puzzled look on the face of a "born Catholic" that now visited church for weddings and funerals, she stopped and smiled.

"You know, trances, asking the dead for good fortune."

Now I was smiling, "Sure, all that normal stuff. So that's where the poodles' names came from. What about her life now, without the nanny? Is she honest, dishonest, or worse?"

Perez looked at me kind of funny. "What do you know that I don't, Tony?"

I quickly retraced my Tuesday lunch with Frank. I started with the burger at Grease he could barely lift, which got a big laugh from Perez, who adores Frank. I went onto the obituary, the tire marks on the funeral home lawn, skipped the details of my chance meeting with Nila, and finished with Emile at the Sailfish Club.

That computer-like mind was quietly taking it all in, with only an occasional nod or frown. As I finished, she said, "Didn't you get involved in a case like that, people being insured, then murdered for insurance? You think it might be a case of that?"

I nodded quietly, not wanting to interrupt her thought process before she came up with something I could use.

She continued, "Her picking up the body is a little strange, and as his fiancée makes it really out there. I might be able to check out the body release being OK'd by Tallahassee; I've got friends in the governor's office."

She paused to take another sip of her coffee and waved to a couple of churchgoers who had just come in from a Saint Edwards mass.

I had held off on the real estate situation because I didn't want to bring up Nila. Perez is like a protective older sister and she knew Nila dumped me for an old flame.

She shook her head. "I can't picture her doing the running over for money part; I expect she inherited plenty. She's a tough operator, but murder for money? Doubt it."

I decided to come clean. "One other thing, turns out Nila's father was in a partnership in a piece of land owned with," and as I spoke I could see her eyebrows rise up a bit, but she kept still, "a guy that was involved with Joan."

She interrupted; I thought to chastise me for Nila, but only to ask, "How involved?"

"We think as a lover, but now that he's dead, she's the executor."

She gave me a stern look. "Where did you get the maybe as a lover idea?"

I was a little taken back by the inflection in her voice, but knowing she's a stickler for fact vs. rumor, particularly in male/female situations, I countered with, "It was thrown out by Nila, who was only guessing."

She gave me that perfect smile. "Let me ask you, Tony, is a woman that manipulates a man by having sex any better or worse than a woman that manipulates by denying sex?"

I was trying to come up with the correct answer, if there is one, and spouted out, "Depends."

She ignored my feeble attempt and continued. "Women who supposedly manipulate, and by the way, it's labeled manipulation when women do it; with men it's called courting."

I wasn't sure if she had finished, but kept still.

She hadn't. "You should understand this, Tony. A woman often has a lot more power when she hasn't slept with the guy pursuing her. Joan, from all I know, is a very strong, attractive woman who does not sleep around to get her way. She has enough going to not have to."

She grabbed my hand. "Lecture over, but now tell me, how can people be dying all around this gal and we cops don't even know anyone is dead. Better not let this get out, or we'll all be fired."

"Your secret is safe with me Perez, as long as you can fix an occasional ticket."

"No problem, Tony. Just pull out Grampy's detective badge and you'll be fine."

Carrie came by with a refill. "How's the acrobat doing, Carrie?"

"He's fine, looks like he'll be getting into that Ringling Brothers school later this year."

"Perez gave me a look. "What's that all about? "

"Turns out her nine-year-old son Nick is incredibly athletic. You know, runs up walls and does back-flips, works out on the trapeze, all that stuff. Seems the circus has a training program for skilled kids who might want to be performers."

"Nice lady, Tony."

"This place has a lot of them."

I got up from the stool, stretched out the kinks from my Ultima workout and sat back down. "So, Sergeant, what's next?"

"One other thing Tony. I don't know all the details, but this Haitian nanny that brought up Joan — seems she died when Joan was in her late teens. The rumor was that the government screwed up the nanny's immigration status. She was legal, but having grown up in Haiti, where Pappa Doc made up the rules as he went along, she both feared and didn't trust the government. Seems she tried to leave the area in a hurry and died in a car crash. Joan took it real hard. If you find someone who knew her during those years, might be something there."

"That's an idea; she grew up in town, so there has to be someone that knew her during that period."

"Well Tony, I'll have a check with my pal at the State House on getting bodies released early, plus see if he knows what's going on with Mecca Farms."

She pushed back her chair and stood behind it. "One other minor detail. What did she do with the body?"

I stood up and gave a "who knows" shrug.

"Come on Perez, I'll walk you to the car. Make sure you don't get mugged."

I opened her driver side door for her, but as she started to slide in, she stopped. "What about this life insurance motive. Have you checked to see if she had coverage on him?"

"Only briefly. I plan to do more, but you seem to think money's not a motive."

She smiled and drove off in her unmarked police car.

CHAPTER 9

Where's the Body?

I sat in my car for a minute, thought about my conversation with Perez, and then called Frank.

As usual, before I could get a word in edgewise, Frankie was talking,

"Heard a good one last night, Tony."

I could tell from the tone he was wound up. Better to wait, as he'd interrupt me anyway.

"Guy comes to work on a Monday with a black eye. Friends ask what happened, and he says, 'There was a very attractive woman standing in front of me in church. Well, she had on this tight silk dress, but in the warm church it was kind of tucked into her fanny, if you know what I mean. I kept looking at it and knew it must have bothered her so I reached over and pulled it out. She turned around and hit me with her psalm book.'"

As usual frank was laughing at his own joke.

"Next week, same thing, comes into work, another black eye.

His friends gather around. 'What happened?'

'You won't believe it,' he says. 'Same woman, same dress, right in front of me.'

'Oh no,' they say, her dress was tucked in again?'

He shakes his head and gives a knowing smile. 'I wouldn't make that mistake again.'

'Why the black eye, they say.'

'Well,' he says, 'the dress wasn't tucked in and I knew she didn't like it that way, so I reached over and tucked it back in for her.'"

It was funny, but I had to wait for Frank to stop laughing at his own joke before I could tell him about Perez.

Finally, the laughing stopped.

"Tony, I've been thinking about Joan picking up the body at the morgue. What did she do, throw it in the trunk? Where did she take it, and in what?"

"Frankie, that's why I'm calling, I had the same idea.

After seeing Emile yesterday I started calling funeral homes to see who might have handled the burial. Bet I called thirty homes, and none of them had heard of Jimmy or Joan. You think she still has the body?"

Waiting for his usual interruption that didn't come, I continued. "Then this morning I had a coffee with Sonja Perez. Seems our friend's thing with funerals comes naturally. Joan had a nanny from Haiti whose entertainment was going to funerals, and she took young Joan along when she was a child. Haitians are Catholic but there's a lot of other stuff mixed in."

"Like what?" His tone finally showed some real interest.

"Like a mild zombie worship, trances, talking to the dead, that kind of stuff. I wonder if she's doing more than just prospecting for real estate sales. Her nanny may have introduced her to some kind of cult, zombie thing."

"We've had this discussion before, Tony. Most children get their beliefs from their parents. Catholic or Protestant, Democrat or Republican, few are converted or have an experience that makes them change, but most accept what they are told. Seems this nanny was like a parent figure. Pretty good chance Joan holds at least some of the same beliefs."

There was a long silence. "Let's go back and see that nice lady at the morgue. I'll pick you up in front of Green's."

My guess was Joan attended a lot of funerals, but would be more apt to visit those of the more prominent Palm Beach families where the houses were bigger. To kill two birds with one stone, so to speak, I cut through the isle at Green's with all the beach stuff and stopped at the checkout counter to pick up the Palm Beach Post.

I headed out to the bench on the corner of Sunrise and North County.

As I sat waiting for Frank, I had to smile at the scene. Here I was sitting on the bench outside Greens, watching parishioners visiting St. Edward's in preparation for the hereafter while leafing through the obituary pages for those already on their way.

Sure enough, there was long write up on Craig S. Deering III, scallywag supreme. His grandfather, extremely wealthy from various business interests across the globe, was a poker-playing confidant of Henry Flagler. He had first come to Palm Beach in pursuit of a Hollywood starlet who later became his fourth wife. Craig, grandson of this fourth and final, idolized his grandfather and, though the times were different, had followed his grandfather's example and spent a lifetime having fun.

After reading the full article, which balanced his exploits with his strong charitable interests in local causes, I gave him a tossup on the hereafter part.

Finally, at the end of the article, I read, "Services today and tomorrow at Quattlebaum Funeral Home on Olive.

I'd been there before. It's a large, first-class facility that caters to all denominations.

CHAPTER 10

Frank Reminisces

As Frank drove, I read him the obituary on Mr. Craig Deering of Palm Beach. Craig's dad had died when Craig was in his mid-twenties. He took over the family business of importing massage oils from Argentina. He turned out to be a natural at the business, and had grown it by ten times by the time he was thirty-five.

He had sold out for more money than you could spend if you lived to be a hundred, and from the comments and condolences of friends, he had apparently tried.

I could tell by Frank's hearty laugh a story was coming.

"I'm surprised he waited this long to leave us. He's younger than I am by ten years, but squeezed a lot in. Probably twenty years ago he and I ended up as partners sharing a golf cart in a member-and-three-guests tourney at Breakers West. The event was on a Thursday morning. By eight that evening four of us, plus his pilot and two extremely well put together flight attendants, were in a limo heading from the airport to the Vegas strip. I think we stayed at the Dunes, which has been since torn down and replaced by the Bellagio. I missed a lot of the party, ended up spending three days and nights with one of Craig's flight attendants."

Frank paused. I could tell he was enjoying the memory. "This girl Sally, with a doctoral degree from M.I.T. in chemical engineering, had put her career of mixing chemicals on hold for few years of mixing drinks. She was making $20,000 a month and all expenses working for her nice 'Mr. Deering.'"

He hesitated again, then looked over and smiled. "She was definitely underpaid."

Frank, whose tall athletic build, quick wit and easy smile attracted a lot of female interest, is old school. He seldom, if ever, talks in detail about his experiences with women.

His stories are more often about his love for his third wife Helene and fond memories of his years with her. A cloud of sadness sometimes follows his stories.

She had been his true soul mate. They had met after his being divorced for many years, and were married on the Greek island of Santorini. They spent ten incredible years together until she succumbed to cancer three years back.

I eat up his rare digressions. I barely knew my own dad, except through my mom's stories. Frank has always been kind of a father figure, and learning anything about his past was always exciting.

I was ready for more detail, but we had pulled up in front of the County Medical Examiner's office — "The Morgue."

Elsa, whose energy level and nifty little figure masked her probable age, appeared as soon as we were announced. This time she gave me a warm two hands on mine hand shake, but greeted Frank with what appeared more than a casual, only the second time we've met, hug. Seemed Frank had called ahead, or more?

Good old Frank, I thought. What's he up to?

She led us through the door that said Private, down a long corridor to a second door, where a four button code let us into to a large room with metal tables. I felt the chill of the cooling system as we entered. To our right, two men in white with surgery masks were working on a body; straight ahead the far wall contained a series of square compartments three-high and four-wide. I guessed where they stored the bodies before and after the procedure we were about to witness.

Elsa turned to Frank and in a surprisingly formal tone, as if giving a tour to two strangers, said, "You were asking about the process we go through here, Mr. Forbes."

Pointing to the men at the table, she recited a lecture I'm sure she had been through many times. "These are the corpses that have been claimed and are being prepared for a formal burial. This procedure is sometimes done here but more often at the funeral home. Drains are inserted into the groin, and the blood is removed. At the same time, a preservative such as formaldehyde is pumped in. The person's eyes and lips are sewn shut. The internal organs are often removed, and a wooden stake is affixed to the spine to keep the body from going into spasms during rigor mortis."

She continued her rehearsed talk, finally turning to the vaults in the far wall, when she continued, "We rarely have more than a half dozen in there; those that never get claimed we eventually incinerate. Not so with your friend. He was taken direct from the vault and given to the couple that picked up the body."

I glanced over at Frank when I heard the word couple. He was clearly having the same thought.

Frank pointed to the side door. "This is where funeral parlors or relatives pick up the body."

"Yes," she said. "It's a loading dock."

As we walked over, a very tall, gangly, long-armed fellow with unkempt gray hair and unusually large hands, standing off to the side, pushed open the double doors.

She addressed him as Adam. "These men were friends of the gentleman who was brought in yesterday, the one who had the car accident."

Adam gave an awkward smile and nodded, but didn't speak.

As we stood on the dock, Frank asked, "Elsa, you are there to sign bodies in and out, so did you happen to notice the vehicle they used to take Jim's body?"

She gave Frank a knowing smile. "Yes, I was curious at the early pickup and made a point of checking. It was a hearse from the Mary Alley hospital. At least that was the name on the side. It was a new name to me."

She held her hands head-high and gave that cute shrug that raised and lowered her ample breasts on that slim frame, making clear what had caught Frank's interest — and ten years older or not, she was getting mine.

She continued, "I checked the yellow pages and there's no such place in the entire state of Florida."

There was a pregnant silence, but not followed by the usual punch line. We just kind of stood looking at each other, each waiting for the other to speak.

Finally, Frank broke the silence. "Elsa, do you know who at the State House gave the OK to release the body?"

She was shaking her head before he finished the sentence.

"Can you find out? I assume this isn't normal procedure."

She waved for us to follow.

As we headed back down the corridor to her office, I asked, "I assume you have been here for some time. No offense, but you don't look like a person I'd expect to meet at the morgue. Whatever attracted you to apply for this job?"

She smiled as though she'd been asked before. "My family owned funeral parlors. I kind of grew up with bodies around the house, so to speak. They had trouble filling the position when my husband died, and I was asked to help out. Here I am ten years later."

Frank was nodding in a way that made me feel he somehow already knew this.

I thought it a good time to ask, "Do you know the Quattlebaum Funeral Home? We are going there next."

"A friend died? I'm sorry."

"No, an acquaintance. We're checking to see if a person with a fascination for funerals might be there."

I couldn't tell from her look or reply whether she knew I was talking about Joan.

"Yes, a fine family, well run home. Ask for Janet. She and I are old friends."

She had been waiting on the phone while we were talking, then nodded, thanked the person on the line and put down the phone. "Might have been someone from Congressman Murphy's office but was really not sure."

I smiled at Frank, "Bingo. Isn't the Mecca Farms property in his district?"

I thanked Elsa for her time, noticing again that Frank's thank you was a lot more personal than mine; it definitely wasn't a goodbye.

CHAPTER 11

Another Funeral

Frank pulled into the parking lot on the south side of the complex. As planned, we got there early.

A short line of people was at the door offering condolences to the family prior to going in. We skirted the line and found seats up front to the right of the casket.

If Joan was planning to speak to the body, we were perfectly aligned to watch.

I whispered to Frank, "What's going on with you and that Elsa? She seems awfully friendly for having met with us once for about 20 minutes."

"Quiet Tony, have a little respect for the dead."

Typical Frank, I thought. He could have seen her six times in the last few days and I'd never know.

As we watched, family members approached the casket first, three kids in the group, probably in their mid-teens, crying their eyes out. I had to smile; I'll bet he was a great Grampy.

They were followed by a group of men close to his age who showed very little of the typical funeral protocol. I guessed they were good friends who appeared to have been out to lunch and had a few drinks, still laughing and telling stories about their dead pal.

If he's somewhere watching, he's probably chuckling along with them.

It got a little slow for a while and then, her head and face wrapped in a dark veil, Joan Diamond approached the coffin. She knelt at the casket, appeared to be saying a prayer, then stood and leaned over the body as though to speak. Her lips didn't seem to move but, still leaning into the casket, she took a small object out from between her breasts and placed it on his chest.

Frank stood up to follow her out.

A little surprised at his seeming disinterest in what she had left in the coffin; I took a step toward the casket to look for myself.

Frank grabbed my arm.

He pointed to his car, "Better to follow her."

Clearly in a hurry, or maybe not wanting to be followed, her red Jag convertible swerved left across the oncoming traffic and into the far lane, causing at least a couple sets of brakes to squeal, then headed north on Federal highway in a big hurry.

"Notice her car Tony. That's a XKRS racing Jag; they run about a hundred forty grand. Remember the wide tire marks on the lawn? That car has 600L 16 racing tires. I noticed it on the way in — super wide. Not a lot of tires like that out there."

By the time Frank had maneuvered the big Caddie safely across and into the north lane, she was a dozen cars ahead.

Knowing Frank's dislike for suggestions concerning his driving, particularly obvious comments like, "you're wasting your time she's too far ahead and, by the way, she's speeding to avoid us or whoever else might be following her," I kept still; then, perhaps stimulated by watching Frank and Elsa, my mind wandered to my brief but pleasant meeting with Nila. What a pliant and cooperative body, I thought, as my fingers, seemingly functioning on their own, pulled out my phone and pressed the speed dial.

"Tony, I've been planning to call you. I had a brief meeting with the Diamond woman."

It wasn't the subject on my mind at that moment, but of interest none-the-less.

"What happened in your meeting with Joan, Nila?"

I had purposely used her name to get Frank's attention, and I switched on the speaker function.

"After talking with Veronica about the potential value if the state develops the area, I doubled the price. Still a good deal for her, but my father will be pleased."

"How did she respond?"

"She was furious. I don't know if she was suspicious that I knew something or that is her normal way of negotiating, but she demanded I wait in her office while she stepped outside with her cell."

Frank was muttering something like "what a bitch" when Nila continued. "Tony, something you might be interested in. There was a half open file on her desk, which I glanced at while I waited. It looked like a list of insurance contracts on a man named Patterson. Something over five million was the total."

I could see Frank mouthing the word bingo.

"Thank you Nila, you are the best! I owe you drinks and dinner. Are you free tonight?"

"Yes Anthony, I'd love to see you. I'll be heading back in a few days. I'm pretty certain Joan will accept. She said she had to check with her lawyer on the land purchase, but I can tell she's interested."

"Great Nila, I'll pick you up at six."

I hung up to Frank's usual comment. "Brings a tear to my eye, the sacrifices in time and money you make for your friend Jimmy."

"What about the policies on Jim, Frankie? You still got that friend in the insurance commissioner's office?"

"Yes, I'll call him tonight at home."

He was shaking his head. "Incredible how hungry these companies are for a little business. There is no way any company should have put a dime of coverage on a down and out street person like Jimmy, but you can be sure they'll be looking closely now that it's a claim. They ought to be liable. He'd be alive if they hadn't issued the policies."

I was nodding in agreement. "Insurance being controlled by the states makes it real cheap for some companies to buy the politicians. Sell anything they want, good or bad."

Frank turned off Federal Highway and crossed the Flagler Bridge onto Royal Poinciana. We passed Sprinkles, RSVP and Main Street

News, all my nice morning friends, finally the building where Mimi the medicine woman had her store and who, sad to say, passed away earlier this year after a long bout with cancer.

My car was in the lot behind Green's. Frank dropped me across the street by the Paramount Theater.

"Tony, I'll call you after I talk with my friend. I'm sure you'll be home early."

I smiled a reply and headed home with visions of a naked Nila dancing in my head.

CHAPTER 12

Emily Confessions

Gabriella released her friend from her hug, stood back and held Emily by the shoulders. "Tell me everything."

She reached for Gabriella's hand, "Come, there is a nice restaurant, Kaffeeklatsch, a bit of a distance from here but the walk will give us time to talk. This place will remind you of visiting your grandmother's kitchen as a child.

Taking Gabriella's hand, she led her out the back of the hotel, through the parking lot and across a green field to the main promenade. They walked and chatted. It was nearing summer and the air was warm in the valley; only the very peaks of the surrounding mountains were still white with snow.

As they passed the Kirchner Museum, Gabriella slowed and pointed to the building where her mother had studied as a young college girl, but noticing Emily's thoughts were elsewhere, she took a quick step to catch up and loop her friend's arm in hers. "Tell me everything about this marvelous man you have met."

Relieved to finally have a friend she could be open with, Emily began. "Arthur and I first met about five years ago in Paris. We were seated together at a lunch at the American Embassy, listening to politicians drone on about nothing. Careful to only be noticed by me, he was feigning falling asleep, and I was trying to keep a straight face. We left the meeting and realized we were staying at the same Hotel de Crillon, which is a block from the embassy. When we sat together at lunch and he had spoken of being stationed earlier in his career in Paris, on the left bank, and of his favorite restaurants, Café de Flore, Deux Magots and Brasserie Lipp. He asked if I'd like to join him for dinner at Deux Magots. We had a wonderful dinner and talked for hours. He was very entertaining, as well as being quite good looking. He had been an aide to General Colin Powell, whom he adored, but was then working for Powell's replacement Condoleezza Rice, whom he only liked. At the end of the evening I was secretly entranced and hoping for more than the polite handshake and kiss on the cheek he diplomatically delivered. We had planned to meet for breakfast early the next morning before our flights.

I woke anticipating our meeting, but got only a brief note stating that he had been called back to Washington. Through friends I later found Arthur had been purged by Cheney, who got rid of anyone who either disagreed with him or knew the inside story of his cherry picking evidence to convince the country to invade Iraq. It was common knowledge that Cheney's twenty years of heart medications had made him so paranoid he even carried a space suit with him at all times for protection against a biological attack. His boss Wilkerson referred to Cheney as a 'lonely, paranoid, frightened Dick Cheney.' Compared to the damage I have seen to our standing with our European friends and allies, that statement is almost complimentary." She put her arm around her friend Gabriella. "Enough about that. Back to the good stuff. I was there in May visiting my mother and went with some old friends for a drink over on St. Germaine."

Seeing the excitement in her face, Gabriella finished the sentence. "And there he was having a drink at Brassiere Lipp."

Emily laughed and hugged her friend. "No, across the Boulevard at Deux Magots. He had taken on a temporary job teaching economics at Princeton, had a vacation and decided to spend some time in Paris."

She paused. "Kismet." Still hugging her friend she started to giggle. "We made love an hour later at his hotel. It was the most beautiful experience of my life. I blush just thinking about it. He was so skilled; while kissing me with such passion, he was rubbing warm oil slowly up, and then slowly back down my inner thighs until I was so hot I thought I would explode. By the time he entered me I had the most incredible orgasm of my life."

She paused, pulled on Gabriella's arm, and looking her straight in the eye said, "Best up until then; I didn't think it could get better, but it did."

Getting a bit unnerved from just listening, Gabriella looked around to see if anyone was near enough to hear. Seeing they were close to their destination, she pointed to the storefront just ahead. "Here we are, Kaffeeklatsch, your choice for the best cakes and lunches in Davos."

Not ready to close her book of memories, Emily threw out one more phrase. "I hadn't had sex in many months, and I got caught up in one night."

They entered an eclectic dining room scene, with furniture in different shades — some modern, some traditional, with cups, saucers and pitchers all different, but somehow fitting perfectly.

Gabriella, whose own sex life had been nonexistent since that episode on the plane, was enjoying her friend Emily's good fortune while feeling both a little envy and somewhat sad about what she was missing. She grabbed her friend's arm. "Come, there is a nice terrace upstairs where we can sit in the sun and talk."

They chatted a bit about the many menu choices, there being a dozen in the coffee section alone. Suddenly, a crash was heard coming from the stairway they had just climbed. Both women instinctively ducked below the level of the table, each watching to see that their friend was safe. The two men at a table by the door got up to look down the stairway just as a very large man in the form of Gabriella's bodyguard, Joseph, appeared.

He waved to the women, "Come quickly, I have a car waiting outside."

They hurried down the stairway past the bodies of two men at the foot of the stairs. He opened the door to the back seat, motioned for them to enter, hurried around to the driver's side, jumped in and sped off.

Watching the women in the rear view mirror, he looked at Emily. "You had warned Ms. Giacometti that members of a rouge splinter group from the south were plotting to try and kidnap her and gain some advantage over the territory."

Gabriella spoke first. "Yes, these are not well educated, nor are they very smart people, but any fool with a gun can be dangerous. We no longer care about controlling the docks in Genoa. Either they don't know it or feel it is less manly to get it without any killing."

She sat back and sighed. "Another reminder of why I should give up this business."

Emily kept silent, letting them deal with their issues. She would deal with hers. She had a responsibility in her position with the FBI to file a report on the deaths she had witnessed, and she was thinking about how she would have one of her subordinates (with close ties to the local police) create a story that did not include Gabriella.

After a prolonged silence, Joseph spoke. "I have a history with these people. Possibly I could make them think I am selling them a territory without your knowledge. Thinking I had betrayed you and sold out a woman would give them a double bonus."

Gabriella nodded, "And put some cash in your pocket, which I would love."

Emily took note at the ease by which this had been achieved — no red tape, no fear of politicians interfering or using it to their political advantage.

She reached her hand out to Joseph, "Thank you for being so alert, Joseph. An incident with us together would be difficult to explain."

Joseph closed the partition and drove on.

Gabriella took Emily's hand. "Perhaps our brief time as school girls talking about boys caught up with us, but this incident forces me to face the reality of my life. I don't know how close I can ever come to normal, but I feel I have fulfilled what my father would have expected of me. I would like to move to the next stage of my life, perhaps become closer to the private citizen he once wished to be."

Emily said, "Of course I would encourage you to pursue your dreams, but who would take over?"

Gabriella nodded to the front seat. Emily smiled her agreement. "I can't have school girl chats with Joseph, but I must agree with the choice."

CHAPTER 13

Nila Brings a Friend

Is the interesting thing about women's gams
those thoughts of bim bam thank you ma'ams?
Or the fantasies that give men's hearts a rush
and often cause the girl to blush?

Nila, in a strapless dress, which was fighting a losing battle to keep her ample breasts in place, greeted me at the door with a hug that quickly turned my thoughts from a cozy dinner at Table 26 into something more immediate.

I had just placed my right arm around her waist and started to pull her close, when I glanced over her shoulder and spotted a gorgeous set of very long legs, only partially covered by a short, tight fitting skirt.

Releasing herself from my surprised grasp, Nila introduced us.

"This is my friend Miranda. She's visiting for a few days from Miami before I head home."

My first feeling was a sense of disappointment. The hug at the door had made me think the dessert might be coming first but, always the optimist, I realized that maybe the game had changed and was now double or nothing. My conflicting thoughts and vivid imagination nearly caused me to miss Nila's introduction.

"Miranda, this is Tony, that cute guy I've been telling you about."

She stood, but instead of extending her arm to shake hands, she held her hand close to her hip, so I had to take a half step closer. With her heels we were eye-to-eye and close enough to feel her warm breath bringing the words.

"Hello Anthony, I've heard so much about you. I feel I already know you."

Her very pale smooth skin was in stark contrast to her jet-black hair, carefully combed to almost cover one eye. She exuded a self-confidence that was both intriguing and almost a little intimidating. The overall impression was a dreamlike 1920's movie star feel that made me want to see another film. But her "Hello Anthony" was followed by a disappointingly cool, firm, almost masculine handshake that made me wonder if we were in competition. For some reason it all combined to make thoughts of the night ahead more than a little interesting.

After a pregnant silence that seemed longer than it was, I blurted out, "All set ladies. I've got us seats at a great bar and restaurant."

We pulled into the crowded Table 26 parking lot and started to exit the car.

My computer pal, Jonathan, who also has the parking concession, gave me a wink of approval when he held the door and watched Nila slide out of the front seat. It changed to a wide grin when Miranda's seemingly endless legs slid slowly, heels first, from the back seat.

Eddie, the maître d and managing partner, hugged us all at the door. Eddie, a class guy, is a major hugger. He led us to the three open seats at the bar.

I had called ahead. Max, the head bartender, had recently returned from a nine-month trip by motorcycle from Mexico to Patagonia. As I suspected, the promise of two attractive women from Argentina, where he had spent over a month, would help to hold the hard-to-get seats at the bar.

He's a big, easygoing guy with a dark crew cut and glasses. He has a beautiful baby daughter, Gabriella, and, as with any proud new father is ready with the pictures for anyone that asks. I suspect he'd give Frank, whose photos of his granddaughter Sophie are so worn you can hardly recognize her, a run for his money.

Max was well prepared and definitely had his priorities straight. Seeing us enter, he came out from behind the bar, gave me a nod of approval and a quick handshake. The girls got a serious hug. He stood looking at the girls for a moment, then dropped his chin and shrugged his shoulders as though preparing to deliver some bad news.

"Se acaba de terminar el Fernet con Coca-Cola, su trago favorito Argentina."

The girls broke into howls of laughter. I stood quietly, wondering what he had said until Nila finally interpreted.

"He said they are fresh out of Fernet and Coke, a very popular Argentine drink."

They were still giggling when Max, now back behind the bar, placed two wine glasses on the bar and held up a bottle of Malbec. "Muy bueno de Mendoza."

For that one I needed no help.

Nila had placed Miranda between us, and soon, thanks to Max's heavy hand, it was working out extremely well. Chatting away in mixtures of Spanish and English, the crowded bar forced the girls to lean close to talk. Since, with South American women, talking often involves moving not just the hands but also the entire body; the evening had the appearance of becoming quite interesting.

Before long we were sharing hors d'oeuvres of beef brisket tacos with red chili sauce and grilled jalapeno-corn salsa. Miranda, energized by the drinks and atmosphere, turned her long legs so they were half straddling mine.

Then, holding a chip with salsa, she said, "Tony, try this," and slowly slid the chip into my mouth, leaving her fingers for me to lick them clean. Her cool smile bordered on a laugh.

She knew she had me.

I glanced toward Nila to see if she noticed. She smiled and winked.

Miranda was first chatting with Nila, and then turning back to me, and with each sip of her drink and burst of laughter, she seemed a little more intimate. First it was just her hand on my knee, then more often on my thigh or around my shoulder.

During interludes of her talking with Nila and my fantasy speculations, I was talking with another Table 26 partner, Dave, my old pal from the Grill. Other men friends, including some I barely knew, were hovering and probably doing their own fantasizing as well.

With the girls chatting in Spanish, and Max pouring the balance of our second bottle of Malbec, my thoughts drifted back to an earlier time.

I was the ripe old age of seventeen, working as a busboy in Boston's North End. Somehow I had lucked out and caught the interest of one of the older waitresses. She had ten years on me in age, and fifty in experience. Needless to say, I was having the time of my life.

We were both off work on this particular Monday night. I had arrived at her apartment looking forward to another night together; perhaps another lesson.

She had ushered me in with a kiss and a hug and, similar to tonight, had an attractive friend visiting. The minor difference was that the friend was another waitress at a restaurant next door, one that I had often admired from afar but never met. We three spent the evening talking, laughing and telling stories. Then, to my surprise, when my friend and I retired to her bed, there was this second, very attractive, completely naked "older woman" in the same bed.

I remember as though it were yesterday. I was lying on my back, with my girlfriend on my right and this second gorgeous woman on my left.

Here is the part I have replayed a thousand times in my mind, fantasizing over and over what might have been.

After lying there patiently for what seemed like forever, I made the error I have regretted ever since.

I rolled over and kissed her friend first.

Max broke my reverie. He was holding up the empty bottle. "Otro trago para el camino." Almost simultaneously, Miranda nodded her approval and her fingertips were gliding slowly across my left thigh.

Sensing a gap between my mind and my mouth, and not sure of what pitch my voice would come out in, I nodded a yes to Max.

I then, very softly, put my hand on hers to let her know it was fine where it was. She turned toward me and smiled. "Thank you for this lovely evening, Tony." Then looking down but leaning close, she whispered, "I know you and Nila were once close and you probably felt deserted when she stayed in Argentina. It was not you. It was to please her father."

Miranda turned on her barstool to face me and very softly continued, "Nila wanted us to meet so you wouldn't be lonely when she left."

I stared to stutter something when she gave my hand a squeeze and smiled, "I'm glad she did."

Max, watching the whole thing, placed a glass of ice water in front of me on the bar.

Not sure he meant for me to drink it or dump it in my lap, I decided on the former and took a sip. Finally, redemption I thought, thirty-five years after rolling over on the wrong waitress.

My reverie was broken when Eddie tapped me on the shoulder and whispered, "Tony, you have a call at the front desk. It's your friend Frank, and it sounds important."

I frowned, slid gingerly off my stool and mustered a, "Thanks, Eddie."

"Tony, glad I caught you. I'm on my way over. You won't believe what I found." Before I could protest, ask what, or explain that I was rather busy repairing a thirty-five year old mistake, he had hung up.

With all his years dealing with the public, reading my expression must have been easy for Eddie. He put his hand on my shoulder, "everything alright, Tony."

"Yeah, fine Edie, thanks," I lied.

I had a feeling Frank's showing up was going to turn my little fantasy back into, well, just that, a fantasy.

Back at the bar the girls were huddled together giggling and whispering in Spanish.

The whispering wasn't for me. My Spanish is limited and normally they speak so fast it wouldn't matter anyway.

But always the optimist, and hoping they were discussing "us," I stood behind them with a hand on each woman's shoulder. Nila put her hand on mine, which I took as a positive, and then listened carefully for the few words I might understand like "dos mujeres y un hombre" (two women and one man). No such luck. Those old standby's, pelo y ropa (hair and clothes) were again the subjects.

Hoping I might catch Frank before he sentenced me to another 35-year wait, I turned my cell back on and headed out into the parking lot. Maybe I could get the story by phone and convince Frank we should deal with it tomorrow.

No such luck. The phone was still ringing when the big Caddie pulled in. To shorten his stay, I jumped in the front seat and pointed. "Pull down the side street to the left. It's too crowded in there."

Frank parked on the quiet side street, just east of the Serenity Garden Tea House, not exactly an appropriate name for my feelings at that point.

He turned in his seat, smiled and announced, "The plot thickens. I got a call from a guy who said he was a retired cop and knows about insurance scams. He's heading out of town early tomorrow and needs to meet tonight."

Frank held up his hand in surrender. "Retired cop. Insurance scams. I think fine. So I suggest we meet at Cucina. He says no, too public. He wants to meet at the Sunset Bar and Grill over in Northwood toward the end of 24th Street."

I sat back trying to focus on Frank rather than the feeling of Miranda's hand on my thigh and the possibility it might never rest there again.

I half listened as Frank described calling Myles and Joanna at Crump in Boston. These two are experts on underwriting insurance on problem cases, and though not involved in this case, have a lot of connections. They were able to find out that a little better than two years back Joan had applied for over ten million on Jimmy. Six was issued; another two million each with Northwestern and Guardian had been rejected.

I smiled and nodded, "Figures, Mutual companies are more interested in protecting their existing clients than making a quick buck for shareholders. Tend to do their serious investigating before they issue, rather than when there is a claim."

Frank continued, "This guy was a retired cop who used to pick up a few bucks as an investigator at one of the services companies they use to check out people they hope to insure. He somehow caught wind of the obituary on Jimmy and remembered the case. Said he couldn't understand this much insurance being applied for on a guy he had trouble even locating, and the ex-cop in him made him keep looking. He happened to bump into Ralph at the West Palm Station. He said Ralph tried to side track him, but he kept pushing and finally said, keep him out of it, but suggested he call me."

Assuming he'd want me along, I said, "Pretty interesting. When are you meeting with him, sometime tomorrow?" I was hopeful.

Frank, I'm sure getting the message from Eddie that I was "busy" with two attractive women, shook his head and smiled. "No Tony, tonight," and adding for emphasis, "tonight at quarter to midnight."

I checked my watch: 10:35.

"The girls are still eating, and then I've got to drive them home. Doesn't sound like you'll need any help. Why don't we meet in the morning at Green's?"

Now, I love Frank like a father, but not when he acts like one. I could see it coming in his look. "Tony, must I remind you that Jimmy, once your very close friend, was probably murdered. Can't you get your mind off poontang for just a couple hours? That Nila dumped you for an old flame back home. It's time to dump her."

I was stuck. I knew anything I said would do nothing but give him more ammunition.

I opened the Caddie door. "I'll take the girls home and meet you there."

Frank's, "Don't be late," wasn't exactly a sympathetic response.

Just to make it even tougher, the girls that I had left alone twenty minutes earlier were hardly visible through the wall of men surrounding them at the bar.

I motioned to Max for the check while trying to put a positive spin on why we were leaving. I leaned in to whisper to Nila, "I've got a lead on your friend Joan Diamond, may help us determine if she actually killed Jimmy. It could work out that you'd be controlling the sale of your dad's property, not her."

It seemed to work.

She gave me a hug. "Thank you Tony, I knew you'd look out for me."

"Yeah, it's best we leave now."

Miranda, now listening in, frowned. "So soon, Tony?"

I smiled as though all was well. "You're staying with Nila tonight, right?"

She gave me a knowing grin, "Yes, of course."

"She has a nice bottle of Malbec in her suite and a big TV."

I held out my hand and crossed my fingers which can be interpreted in two ways:

1) I have a very short meeting with Frank and an investigator (white lie)

2) I'll drop you and be back before you get the bottle opened (hoping for luck).

By the time they finished hugging goodbyes to Max, Eddie, and everyone else at the bar, plus driving them back to the hotel, I was, of course, already late.

I escorted them to the door, kissed each softly on the lips and headed to the car.

In spite of appearing to put pleasure first, I was, in fact, very interested in what this fellow had to say.

No the conflict gams create, dear sir
is though together they can stir
a man to sometimes lose his heart
what he really wants is them apart.

CHAPTER 14

Voodoo Palm Beach Style

It was ten of twelve. A quick left and an immediate right took me over the Flagler Bridge on the fly. The Flagler's quarter to and quarter after schedule fit perfectly as it always provides an excuse to be late. "Damn bridge was up."

The Sunset Grill is about a half mile north down Dixie at the end of the second block of 24th. It's got great prices, excellent food, and a half local, half out of town clientele. It borders on a nice — and becoming nicer area. When I first found it three or so years ago, I thought it was new, but it had already been there for six or eight years. The section has had some booms and busts, but is doing well again.

I drove by and around the corner, found a parking space and then elbowed my way through the crowd at the small bar.

It took a minute to adjust to the light, but I finally spotted Frank in a rounded leather booth in the back corner of the semi-dark restaurant section.

He waved me to a seat and beat me to the punch. "Bridge up?" came with a sarcastic smile before saying, "Tony this is Vinnie Carangelo; he's got a very interesting story."

The retired cop description had set me up for something other than this surprisingly attractive guy, who was still quite young. He had jet-black hair, a perfect smile, and I guessed him to be of Italian descent.

I smiled and held out my hand. "Lieto di incontrarvi. Da dove vieni?"

He stood and shook my hand. "Nice meeting you as well, Tony. I'm from Chicago. Was a cop there for fifteen years. Came down here to get out of the cold. Been doing odds and ends, which is how I hit upon this insurance scam."

I sensed an air of confidence that probably came from growing up, as I did, in a close-knit Italian neighborhood.

I waved away the waitress, still hoping to keep it short and get back to the girls.

Frank said, "Vinnie thinks we have some sort of zombie voodoo thing going on. Tell him Vin."

"As you know, Ms. Diamond was cared for by a Haitian woman. Probably her ancestors were brought there from Africa along with their beliefs, one of which is that with the correct rituals, connections can be made with deceased family members. Most Haitians are now Catholics, but old beliefs remain. Many Haitians somehow combine the two."

He hesitated, seeing my distracted look, which to him looked like, "It's late, I'm tired, get to the point," but was actually my split vision of Nila's breasts fighting to jump out of her strapless dress and Miranda's long legs coming slowly out of the back seat.

At any rate, he finally got to the point.

He held up two fingers. "First, in order to maintain contact with the person in the afterlife, you need to comply with various death rituals including constant maintenance of the tomb. This will make it difficult for whoever killed Jim to hide his body, since they must continue to visit."

He hesitated when he saw my look. "Tony, we don't know for certain Joan Diamond killed him. We only really know for sure she picked up the body."

I shrugged in agreement — at least to the "she picked up the body" part.

He continued. "We don't know if this is the direction they took, but it is a possibility they have created a zombie."

I stood and stretched. "No disrespect, Vinnie, but this vampire business is kids' late night TV stuff. You don't need me in this conversation. I'm a definite non-believer."

Vinnie stood and put an arm on my shoulder. "Hear me out Tony. There is a side of truth to this. Have you ever heard of sex slaves?"

"Sure, young girls drugged or addicted become captives of their pimp, or the drug itself."

He continued. "This is similar but more extreme. One of the drugs they use is venom called tetradoxine, found in several species of puffer fish. This stuff causes the body to go rigid; the person's limbs stay in the same position with no response to outside stimulus. It causes a complete loss of muscle control. All bodily functions such as breathing are slowed down. In the extreme they seem dead but are somehow still aware of what goes on around them."

I interrupted him. "You think Jimmy is still alive? I mean, he was hit by a car."

Vinnie smiled, "The Diamond broad picked up the body before they could do an autopsy. We don't really know."

Frank was nodding like he knew something I didn't.

I smiled at him and wagged a finger. "How do you already know this stuff? A bit of pillow talk with Elsa?"

Frank pointed to Vinnie, "Let him finish, Tony."

Vinnie took a sip of his Stella. "In Haiti, people have been buried for dead and then dug up and given an antidote by a sorcerer, a person they call a Bokor. The trick is to only give them enough antidotes so they barely function — just enough to take orders. They're aware of what goes around them, but can't think or act on their own. They make slaves of them. They become what we think of as zombies and use them to work in the fields, or with women they rent out their services."

"You mean they could give them enough antidotes to bring them all the way back?" I said.

Vinnie shrugged his shoulders and held out his hands. "Jimmy could be alive or dead. Could be buried or hiding out somewhere. All we know is Joan will soon be six million richer, with not a lot of downside."

I smiled. "Right you are. No body for a potential murder rap. No relative or heirs poking around for the proceeds. Insurance companies hate publicity and are only interested in getting their money back. The risk of them pushing it beyond that is small."

I thought for a minute as Frank and Vinnie were commiserating about money-hungry insurance companies. "Hey guys, you think this Jimmy on the skids was a set up?"

Frank said, "Don't know for certain. I haven't seen him in some time. He was drinking a lot after that bitch with the hot body faked getting beat up and then extorted and stole most of his money. Joan hooked up with him somewhere in the middle of his descent."

I looked at Vinnie. "What's next?"

He stood up, waved to the waitress and handed her a credit card. "I don't know about you guys, but next for me is the bed. I've got a seven o'clock flight to Chicago to see an old girlfriend."

I drove back across the bridge, thinking about my old pal Jimmy. Was he dead, halfway dead, dead once, now alive? Vinnie's story about zombie's was somewhat convincing when he was there telling it, but the more time I put between us, the more I began to question it.

Too much work for a fried brain at one-fifteen in the morning. I decided to deal with something more immediate, though equally as complicated, but at least a place where I'd had a modicum of experience.

I took a left off the bridge, then a quick right and stopped in front of the Bradley Hotel. I was hoping for a glimmer of light in Nila's window. Pitch black.

A car's headlights brought me out of my fantasy.

Not wanting to get arrested as a peeping Tom, I stepped on the gas and headed home while my tired brain was trying to calculate how old I'd be in another thirty-five years.

CHAPTER 15

Starbucks with Elsa

Who knows what triggers our thought process, but coming that close to a double header was probably a good starting point.

In my half-awake dream, Gabriella was lying next to me. It was pitch dark but I could feel the softness of her thighs and breasts through her soft silk slip. She was kissing my cheek, then my neck. This went on for what seemed like somewhere between an eternity and a few seconds.

I listened to what sounded like her low whisper.

It was the phone.

Tony, I'm having coffee with Elsa at quarter of eight. Can you make it?

The clock on the bureau said 7:14.

"Where?"

"Starbucks on Clematis. She contacted me early this morning. Something's come up."

I was going to ask if her early morning contact was a tap on the shoulder, but instead murmured, "Sure," and hung up.

Starbucks is daytime Clematis. Across from Grease and Duffy's, two great sports bars with their dozens of TV's. It's squeezed in between Rocco's Tacos and Design Within Reach. It opens officially at six a.m., only a few hours after the kids' late night dance places close, and closes a few hours before they open.

The women at Starbucks are a younger version of the girls at Green's — first class all the way.

Elsa and Frank were seated to the left of the door. She waved, Frank grinned.

I tried not to grin back. Damned if that boy's not in love.

I pointed to the counter at the far end on the left, meaning I'll get a coffee and join you. I passed Jen, the hardest worker on the street, down on one knee putting the day's sandwiches and other goodies in the chest. If you come early enough, either Jen or manager Daniela will be out scrubbing the sidewalk, then putting out the tables for the smokers. Daniela, in her tenth year with Starbucks, has a gorgeous smile and beautiful thick black hair that you only see if you get there early before she ties it up for the long, busy work day.

By the way, don't get any ideas; her boyfriend is very good-looking, and very big. Stephanie, who works here, is raising two kids and taking courses in biology. She took my card for the venti half-café. The very cute Shannon with a new curly hairdo was pouring. I commented on Shannon's hair and asked Stephanie, "How's Zoey." Out came a photo of her high-spirited four year old.

I often think how each of the people we touch, even for a moment, has a whole life of their own with their own joys and problems.

Elsa, sitting up very straight in the booth next to Frank, had on a bright red jersey that looked like it was painted on. She had done something different with her hair since I had seen her at work. I'd try and describe the new 'do, but that's definitely not my area of expertise. Enough to say she looked great. Apparently it wasn't just Frank who was smitten. I gave her a kiss on the cheek and sat facing the young lovers.

Elsa spoke first. "I was telling Frank that after you two came by the other day, one of the assistants in the lab, Adam, the fellow who opened the door to the loading dock when you were there, asked me about you. He said he might have seen your photo in the Shiny Sheet regarding some investigation or something. It seemed a little strange;

he's the last person who would be interested in who makes the pages of a paper on Palm Beach society. I told him you were a friend of the fellow Jim Patterson who was hit by a car the day before.

He came into my office later and brought it up again, kind of talked around the subject. Seemed what he really was interested in was if I knew the body was taken out before there were any real tests done. Then something interesting happened."

Elsa was a good storyteller. She stopped to sip her coffee, solidifying my interest. "I told him I knew Patterson was dead, but didn't have a scratch on him — no cuts or bruises — none of the normal things you'd see after a car accident.

"He seemed surprised I knew, but only said, 'Oh, yeah,' as though to pass it off."

I was thinking about Vinnie's zombie tale. It was somehow becoming a little more believable.

Frank put his arm around her shoulder and gave Elsa a little hug. "There's more."

She gave me a knowing smile. "Later he asked if I knew of others where there were few outward signs of trauma, other cases where the bodies were picked up before an internal exam. I said I wasn't sure."

I asked the obvious, "Were other stiffs picked up by Diamond, after a call from some politician?"

"Possibly, but who or what politician authorized the release seems to have been purposely confused. Adam was going to check back at the records. Was almost like he might have already known, was more interested in what I knew."

I looked over at Frank, "Are they only pretending to kill people for the insurance, and then bringing them back to life, maybe splitting a piece of the insurance before sending them out of the country? Or just creating an army of zombies for some other weird reason?"

Elsa was shaking her head. "To be honest, I wouldn't trust anything handled by the state or the feds."

Up came her first finger. "As far as the state goes, a couple years back, our well run state was the leader in dispensing OxyContin, otherwise known as hillbilly heroin. Broward County had more "pill mills" than McDonalds. It got up to over 1,000 pain clinics in the state before they noticed and did anything about it; probably created thousands of new addicts."

Up came the second finger. "The feds have done many medical experiments over the years. I don't know if you remember that White Coat experiment on conscientious objectors to Vietnam. Many were fine after undergoing some weird stuff, but some wished they'd gone to 'Nam instead. There are many cases of this going on over the years. No president or party is immune. In 2010-11 the government put out a flu vaccine that hadn't even been tested. It was limited to a few cities, but people thought they were getting the tried and true. Maybe some drug company with government covert backing is creating a group for testing drugs and vaccines? The follow up on these people that they've used as guinea pigs is somewhere between very lax and non-existent."

She stopped and rolled her eyes, then in a slightly higher pitch, added, "Plus, the politics."

I was beginning to really like this girl. She's done her homework.

"Frankie, you had an assistant years ago who spoke Mandarin Chinese, was hired by one of the big companies as an interpreter when China was just opening up to the outside world. What did you call her, Weissie, Leslie Weiss?"

Frank smiled. "Nicest girl, smart as a whip. She went to U Conn. Loved languages and had gone through every course in the school but Mandarin, so she took that too. Come to think of it, she was interviewed before and after China by the CIA. She eventually left me, and might have gone to work for them. It was difficult to get much out of her. China was doing a lot of experiments on real subjects then, probably still is, but that was a long time ago." Frank was spinning the dial on his iPhone. "I still get cards, occasional calls."

He stood and slid out from behind the table. "Let me go outside to get better reception. It's a long shot, but maybe she knows something."

I smiled at Elsa. "Seems you and Frank have a lot in common."

A blush and, "Yes, we do," was all I got.

"Elsa, this fellow in the lab, Adam, that told you about other possible fake death situations. Is he a pretty reliable guy?"

She gave me a surprisingly sly smile. "For sure. I've known him forever. He worked for my family when they had the funeral parlors. He's very smart, has advanced degrees in astronomy, but is so kooky he can only deal with the dead. I never got the details and he won't discuss it, but I believe his parents were killed in a car crash when he was quite young, which may have something to do with it."

"He's just fascinated by death."

She hesitated and smiled. "Describes life as, 'a brief stop in the endless abyss of eternity.'"

Brief stop in the endless abyss of eternity, I thought. I like it.

"I got him the job at the morgue, a perfect place for him." She was giggling to herself as she spoke.

"At the morgue he can discuss life in the hereafter with the dead."

Her laughing stopped. "My concern with this whole deal is that the calls from the State House may be initiated by someone higher up."

"Like what," I said.

"Like the feds. As I said, they've run all kinds of experimental programs over the years on mind control with everything from LSD to hypnosis, prolonged torture, or even sexual abuse.

It started after World War II. Seems they thought the Germans and others had developed techniques to not just control people, but to actually read minds. Believe me, once our defense department got into the act, this stuff went right on up through the Iran-Contra scandal."

She hesitated as though to control her anger. "Iran-Contra, by the way, also involved trading drugs for arms and some pretty horrific experiments on real people."

I had to ask, "Where do you get all this stuff, and how do you know what's real and what isn't?"

"I told you I was widowed ten years ago." She dropped her eyes and fingered her coffee cup. And then, without looking up, said almost in a whisper, "My husband was CIA. Died overseas on assignment. I was never told the cause of death."

"What was he working on?"

"Don't know. To protect me he had never gotten into details of his work." She looked up and appeared to be trying to smile her way out of an uncomfortable feeling then said.

"Did you ever read Billie Budd?"

"Sure, Billie's innocent but takes the rap for the good of the system — in that case the British Navy."

"When I found my husband's will it was tucked into the pages of Billie Budd, right after the trial where Budd has been executed. The will was in the pages where his guilt is questioned. It was like he wanted me to know something."

She paused. "I think these weird experiments were an area that my husband was involved. He seemed very troubled by his assignments prior to his death."

"You think your husband was murdered?"

"They called it an accident, but I've always wondered."

Wanting to know more, but get away from the discomfort of having to talk about her husband, I asked, "You have clearly spent a lot of time thinking and researching this stuff. Do you think Jim is a zombie?"

She laughed. "No. That zombie stuff is movie and books crazy talk."

She shrugged. "That said, our government has been experimenting for years with people and drugs. Then there are some people whose backgrounds with abuse have caused them to repress their past to such an extreme they are a clean slate, others retain several personalities to escape the horror of their lives. Maybe people like your friend Jim Patterson fall into the same category without undergoing the bad stuff to get there?"

"Yeah," I said, "if you don't consider being sent to the morgue as a dead body with the possibility you may not get picked up and brought back to life before you are buried alive." I hesitated. "As bad stuff."

She nodded and laughed, "My husband told me about drugs they use to get people to tell the truth, drugs that make people obey commands. Guess you could connect that to a zombie thing."

My friend Arthur, former radio guy from western Mass., a big Boston sports fan, patted me on the back on his way by the table. He gave me a "go Bruins" thumbs up.

I waved and continued. "So you think Joan is making her money from the insurance, but calming her conscience by saying it's to aid the CIA in their quest to save mankind?"

She was looking up and smiling at Frank, who had finally came back from his phone call. "Any luck?"

Frank threw his long legs and broad shoulders back in the padded bench next to Elsa. Then, seeing Elsa's hands folded on the table, placed a big paw over her hands, gave a little squeeze and started in. "Weiss threw another angle at me. She said it was not her area, but knew agents that were involved in those mind control games, and guessed the games were still going on."

It appeared from Elsa's nod at the mention of mind control that she and Frank had already had this discussion.

Frank continued. "She suggested I check on a woman here in Palm Beach who was recruited out of high school in Texas, in the late '90s. She had a photographic memory and an uncanny ability to pick up languages. Weiss met her later during a trip to China. She said this woman, Stacey, works at the Main Street News in Palm Beach and may still do some work for "Big Brother" on an as needed basis. She has a sister named Rebecca, also very smart, who may or may not do some CIA stuff as well. Works at a place called Clematis Street Books. Isn't that the variety store down the end?"

I leaned in. "If it's the woman at the front counter, I have spoken to her many times. Very pleasant lady, but never would have suspected."

Frank, grinned. "You should have spoken to her in Chinese."

Elsa stood up from the table. "Excuse me boys. I'm going down to say hi to this China doll."

Frank started to get up. I stood and grabbed his arm. "Let her see what she can find out on her own. This Rebecca might open up to another woman, particularly one whose husband was CIA"

I grabbed my cup. "I'm getting a refill. You OK?"

He nodded.

Daniella was at the counter working as a team with Shannon.

I held up the two cups, and before I could speak, Daniella gave me that great smile. "Venti half-café and a regular dark."

"Does either of you ladies know Rebecca, who works at the Clematis News?"

Shannon nodded. "Not well, but enough to talk with once in a while. Nice lady."

I stood waiting for more, and when it didn't come I asked, "She there every day? I mean, ever seem to disappear for a while?"

Shannon gave me a funny look, like where we going with this? But I got the answer I wanted. "She's gone for a day or so. I think she's got a sick mother over on the other coast she looks after. Last fall she was gone for about a month."

"Thanks ladies."

When I got back to the table, Elsa was still missing.

Frank said, "Tony, what about that woman with the FBI you met in Paris when you were chasing after Gabriella. Ever reconnect with her?"

The name Gabriella gave me a little pang. "We exchange notes once in a while. She plays it pretty close to the vest, never much beyond the weather and hope you're well. Nothing on Gabriella. I did have her private line in Paris. I sense she's pretty negative on some of the political stuff that gets mixed up in her job. If the feds are involved, this might be one of those negative areas where I could get her talking."

I looked up to see Elsa heading toward the table. "Any luck?"

Elsa plunked herself down and leaned comfortably into Frank. "I got a little lucky. When I entered the store she was busy at the counter so I looked around and found one of those occult magazines, Evolutions Gate. I waited until she was free, then walked toward her very slowly so she could see what I was reading.

"She bit. I told her I worked at the county Morgue, was interested in rituals. She got right into it, is hot on the occult. She started to get busy at the register and said she gets out at five and asked if I'd like to meet for a drink."

Frank was beaming like a proud father and wearing a big smile. "She's going to put you out of work, Tony."

She continued, "I hadn't got to asking about Leslie Weiss, so I stood reading my Evolutions Gate until she was free, then approached her again. She gave me a strange look like what did this have to do with the occult, but then gave a wide smile of remembrance when I asked if she knew Leslie. She said she had met her couple of times, but through her younger sister Stacey, who runs the bookstore at Main Street News. I explained that Leslie had worked for my friend Frank and had suggested we meet and that Leslie might have mixed up which sister worked where."

"She opened up again with very general stuff. Said she's no longer involved. I asked about her sister's involvement and she said, 'You better ask her.' She did reiterate that her sister Stacey went to China and she had worked with Leslie, but wouldn't get into details about what they did.

"As she explained, for a couple of little girls from small town Texas, the money was a lot better than clerking in the local drug store, so she signed on and a few years later got a job infiltrating so-called radical groups, like protestors at the 2000 Republican convention in Philadelphia, or the 2008 convention in St. Paul, Minnesota. Basically, any group that someone in the government considered radical. Most cases it was just people that didn't agree with those in power. While I was with her at the counter, she called her sister and asked if she was free for a drink after work. I'll get a chance to talk to them both."

I stood and held out my hand. "Great work Elsa. Call me if you find out anything from Stacey. I sort of know her, but only as the nice woman who works at the News store. I am very friendly with her boss Briana who manages the store. She's Italian, a very pretty brunette, always smiling, and a great cook. Customers love her. She runs a tight ship."

As I crossed the Flagler Bridge onto Royal Poinciana I found myself sitting in traffic across from where I had first spotted Nila.

I had a thought.

No, for you readers who only have sex on your minds, it wasn't about the two women probably still asleep at the Bradley. That's a "strike while the iron is hot" situation and too much time had passed.

My thoughts were, quite naturally, all business.

I wondered why, on our first visit to the morgue, had Elsa decided to show two guys she had never met that Joan Diamond had signed the form to release Jimmy's body?

Did she suspect there was a problem and was looking for some help? Maybe, but why us? Her husband was CIA, so she must know others in government. She had jumped at the chance to meet with Rebecca, who apparently had also worked for the CIA. Did she have a combined agenda — the death of her husband and this body-snatching business? Seemed pretty long odds they could be related. My guess was there was more she hadn't revealed.

Or maybe it was simple — she liked Frank. I hoped for his sake that part was real.

Just as I pulled into Sunrise, my cell buzzed. It was Sonya. "Tony, I picked up a little dirt you might use in this Joan Diamond deal."

"Great, Perez, free for an early lunch?"

"I'm at Nick and Johnnie's. Come on over."

CHAPTER 16

Nick and Johnnie's

It was still early. Taylor, a tall, slim, attractive young woman with jet-black hair and cool glasses, was whispering and giggling with her pal Ashley.

As you might expect, even the waitresses and bartenders in Palm Beach are first class; Nick has a good eye; Ashley will finish up her master's degree in marketing this June before she heads back to Chicago for a job in advertising. Taylor works two jobs, nights as bartender at Buccan, and days as waitress at Nick and Johnnie's. Her real passion and future will be as a designer of fashionable women's suits.

Perez, a head turner herself, was waving from an outside table to the far right.

An avid reader, she had her usual three newspapers spread out on the table. Her morning ritual ran a little later today than normal — to check in with her friend Briana at Main Street News to pick up local chatter and the Wall Street Journal. She likes to keep up with her husband, a senior vice president at one of this little town's many major banks. She also reads the Palm Beach Post and our own Palm Beach Daily News for the photos and fluff.

The Daily News was opened to a page with a dozen photos of major givers at benefits. And there was Joan, standing with three men. One was my pal, Emile DuPont. I knew she was his client, but a date? She looked great, but in her early 50s is about twenty-five years north of Emile's female sweet spot.

I turned to Perez. "What's this all about?"

"Tony, look. Check out the benefit. American Haiti Fund, and see this fellow beside her with the big ears? He's a top aide to Governor Scott, very connected, first name basis with Charlie Crist, Jeb Bush — anyone in Florida politics."

With her finger on the photo she slid it over to the third gentleman in the group and started laughing, "Tony, this guy is a prime example of the old saw, 'If you don't get caught you haven't done it.'

He comes from up your way, North of Boston, I think Lynn. He's at all the benefits, a big contributor who's entertained and fawned over. Story is he got his start by insuring the building of his failing business for three times its value, and then burned it down."

'Don't tell me Perez. I bet I can guess the trick."

She folded her arms and sat back, "Ok smarty, go ahead."

"It's easy. Set a small fire with a short in the electrical system, and then pack the thermostat to the sprinkler with dry ice. By the time the ice melts, the fire is out of control, the ice is now water, and nobody is the wiser."

"Very good Anthony. Go to the front of the class. Growing up in Boston's North end, you probably had a few friends who used that very trick."

"Did indeed. Of course they haven't all survived. But this guy didn't make all his money burning down buildings, so how did he make enough to be standing next to a DuPont?"

"Easy. Embezzling. The feds are rarely able to prosecute for embezzling. They get them on not paying taxes. Tax avoidance is a major crime and much easier to prove and prosecute. He understood the rules and took the extra step. Paid the tax on about twenty million and walked."

Taylor brought me a coffee. As I watched her walk away I got a jab from Perez. "Too young for you."

"I know Perez, but the more important reality is this: if we ever got close, she'd probably want to fix me up with her favorite aunt, her mother's older sister."

"So Tony, speaking of friends, what's the latest with your pal Jimmy?"

I wasn't sure what to reveal. We have a close relationship. I tell her what I know right up to the edge of what might compromise her position as a police officer. When she shakes her head I stop.

I told her about Jimmy's body, corpse, whatever, being free of external bruises. I skimmed through my coffee discussions with Elsa, her interest in government interrogation programs and her husband being CIA, but left out Rebecca and Stacey. I felt I should respect her privacy unless it mattered.

"It doesn't make any sense, Tony, particularly the Joan part. I have spoken to several guys at the station and others who know her. She's about as tough as they come in business, but apparently gives a lot of money to help kids in the Latin, not just Haitian community. It's all very hush hush. Except for this Haitian charity in the paper, she avoids any publicity to an extreme. Plus, she comes from lots of it. Just can't see someone like that killing people, especially for money."

"Maybe they aren't dying?"

She stood up from her chair. "Maybe not. I have another close friend at the State House. I'll try again."

She handed her ticket to the valet and walked back toward me. "Joan used to be a regular at the Palm Beach Grill, maybe still is. Why don't you talk to your friend Rebecca? Maybe she has some hint of what Joan is really about."

"Good idea. I'll head over at five, before they get busy."

The Grill, where I first saw Gabriella, also reminded me of Frank's question, "What about that woman with the FBI, the one you met in Paris?"

I sat quietly for a moment. Gabriella. Beautiful, soft Gabriella. It had been over two years now, but it felt as clear as yesterday. Every image, every touch, ready to pop out if I let it; flirting with her image in the mirror at the Grill, meeting her at Mrs. Fisher's party, then later at 32 East. Her house, where our thighs first touched as we sat on her couch looking at photos of her family in the scrapbook as she told me the story of her life. The first time we made love and her prophetic comment, "Slow Anthony, slow. Our love can't last. Give me memories." I was neither listening nor paying attention to her words. I should have. Would I ever see her again?

"Mr. Tauck." The voice seemed far off at first, as it broke through my reverie. I looked up. It was Ashley with a pot of coffee pointing to my cup. Looks like you need this. Then with a smile, she said, "You know we charge room rates for napping."

I sat for a bit sipping my coffee, trying to clear thoughts of Gabriella and focus on Jimmy and Joan. What was their real relationship? It wasn't just that he was older and more than a little run down — no pun intended. But I was beginning to guess that Joan wasn't his type either. Was the connection a simple "insure a down and out guy to collect on his insurance"? Possible. It happens more often than you think.

About a block into my two-block trip home, I thought of Kate.

It was just after twelve. Maybe I could catch her before she left for lunch.

"Katherine. Guess who?"

"What do you mean guess who? It's that good for nothing playboy who never calls his oldest friends."

"I just called. Free for lunch?"

"Yes, but it's going to cost you."

"Oh?"

"Chez Jean-Pierre, 12:30 at the bar."

"See you there."

CHAPTER 17

Kate at Chez Jean-Pierre

After Starbucks and Nick and Johnnie's, hunger wasn't on my list of complaints, but the best French restaurant in a very rich town was a great choice. Even when you're not hungry, this menu will get you there. Imagine scrambled eggs with caviar, Dover sole meuniere, or a taste of beef bourguignon.

Kate tells me to call her the more formal Katherine when I haven't called for a while, and I hadn't. She's a long-time very good friend that has been a lot more, until she finally got smart and drew the line. She managed through working two jobs and a lot of salesmanship to get four kids through college and into good lives — without much help from her two ex-husbands. She moves easily between the wealthy clients of her hotshot attorney boss and the people who work for a living to keep the town functioning. There's a network of people who work in restaurants, offices, or who sell real estate and have a handle on about everything happening in town, with a focus on who's doing what to whom.

Kate is well liked, connected, and knows when to talk and when to keep her mouth shut. If there were something going on with Joan, she would possibly know.

Chez Jean Pierre is in the block between Royal Poinciana and my place on Sunrise. I had a few minutes, so I decided to drive home, leave the car and walk back.

Eli, the Mr. Fix-it in our complex, saw me, waved and came over. "I don't know if there's anything to be concerned about Mr. T, but I saw a fellow on the front lawn who seemed to be looking through the bushes into your place."

"Did James tell you about the guy checking out my car in the parking lot?"

He nodded, "Probably the same guy."

"Thanks Eli. I've got to meet someone and I'm late. Can we talk later?"

Kate was chatting away with the very attractive bar tender, a red head with a serious front porch, she introduced as Rusty.

While I ordered a pinot noir, she picked up her Moet, and headed to her table opposite the bar.

"You never used to drink those for lunch."

"Do now, and I'm planning on several."

"Really?"

"I know what you're going to ask me and it may take some time."

I laughed and held up my glass. "I'm all yours."

She tipped her glass against mine and started in. "Truth is we've been dealing day and night with a big corporate case and just cleaned it up. Ted, my boss, has been telling me to take some time off, unwind. So here I am."

She took another sip. "I know that Frank has got a crush on the Norwegian broad at the morgue. I know your pal Jimmy was hit by a car, and I know you were seen at Table 26 flirting with an old girlfriend." She paused and held up her glass again for emphasis, then downing the rest said, "And her friend from Argentina."

She was shaking her head, "Tony, you had that woman from Italy you were mooning over for months after she left. God knows where she is, but if she's the one for you, go after her. What are you doing out with all these bimbos?"

I certainly wouldn't classify Nila as a bimbo, but that was an argument for another day.

"Wow! Were you were saving that up or what?"

I waved to Rusty, who had looked over when Kate raised her voice. "Two more of the same, please."

"Tony, you've been my friend for many years and I care about you. I just wanted to get it off my chest before I go about solving one of your crimes for you."

I poured the remainder into the new glass. "What do you know about Elsa, who Frank is gaga over?"

"I know you shouldn't trust her. She plays a Miss Goodie Two-Shoes, but she's not. Word is she's been involved with one of the other guys at the morgue for years."

My ears perked up on that one. "Is she still? How many years? Since before her husband died? What do you know about him?"

She was nodding. "The morgue guy's a little weird, but so is she." She was smiling and leaned forward. "Rumor is he's off into some weird cult shit. She can't be far behind."

I moaned. "Jesus, I hope not. Frank is like a teenager in love for the first time."

She leaned back in her chair and held out her hands. "Hey, I'm just the messenger. Maybe my info is old. I could be wrong. Maybe she loves Frank and ditched the other guy. All I'm saying is she may not be the sweet little innocent she seems. She and her supposed CIA dead husband."

"What are you talking about? He wasn't with the government? She told me he was working on some secret project and died mysteriously."

"Tony, truth is I don't know. I just don't have a good feeling about her or anything she says. But let's talk about the rumors I've heard. You know up until recently when the feds cracked down, Florida was the pill capitol of the world. Thirty-two million pills in the first six months of 2010 cut to a million in the next six after the feds finally moved on it, closed down 400 clinics, and put about 80 doctors in jail. Oxycodone clinics were everywhere — more sold here than the rest of the country put together, by a lot. It's still going on because there are a lot of people still hooked, but now they are bouncing between pharmacies to get as much as they need.

The word is that some of these pill mill guys that didn't get caught have graduated to another area."

She stopped for emphasis. "The procurement and sale of body parts."

"Are you crazy? That's overseas stuff, you know: Niger, Bangkok. People are desperate to feed their family and will sell a kidney for a year's wages. Or people just kidnapped and cut up. But not here in the states!"

She laughed, "Where have you been, big guy? You can sell your blood for twenty-five bucks."

I nodded.

She continued, "Women sell their eggs, rent their womb, and now guys can sell their sperm."

She held up her glass. "Think of all that sperm you wasted Tony, plus all the money you spent getting women to accept it."

We were both laughing now as Rusty brought, I hoped, a final drink.

As Rusty put down her Moet, Kate asked, "Rust, you ever heard of the sale of body parts?"

"You bet, Kate. Big business." She started toward the bar and then turned toward us, throwing out her chest and laughing. "What do you think I could get for these?"

I was going to say, "Serious money," but held my tongue.

Kate pointed to Rusty. "She's 100 percent American Indian, Apache. Her father was a chief."

Kate was wound up. "What is the limit, Tony, and who sets it? Politicians who are influenced by money? The Catholic Church or some Evangelical group that doesn't believe in evolution or science? It's my kidney; I can sell it if I want to. Believe me, this stuff is going on. The problem is, who's a willing donor and who's an addict or drunk that's being cut up against their will?"

I was nodding and starting to see her point. The fact that Kate had a hot little body and was a great kisser was somehow getting into the mix. The wine was bringing back some memories and I was imagining her sitting there naked.

I had to focus.

I hadn't planned to get this far into it with Kate, but she seemed to know more than I did, so I asked.

"Kate, what do you know about zombies, or zombie worship?"

"I know it's an island thing. A lot of the Haitians and others originally taken there as slaves from Africa brought those beliefs with them. Though most got converted to Catholicism, they kept a lot of the old stuff. But I don't hear much about it."

I had originally called her to see if she knew anything about Joan and had gotten a lot I hadn't bargained for. Kate excused herself and headed to the ladies room.

I'd been thinking about Frank. I couldn't tell him outright, plus maybe her involvement with the co-worker was history. Better to wait and get more facts before I took any action, not that I had the slightest idea what that would be.

I waved to Rusty for the check.

As she placed it on the table, she asked, "Aren't you in that miracle granting condo down the street?"

I handed her my credit card and gave her a bewildered look.

"Yeah," she said, "One of the guys who works at the desk was telling a friend he had a new place and went shopping for sheets, pillows — all the bedroom stuff. He was complaining about how he had to wait; it was too expensive. Next day, the same two guys are in the parking lot and heard all this yelling, a big fight between the couple on the second floor. All of a sudden a bedspread comes flying out the window, followed by sheets, pillows — everything but the mattress. Turns out they were moving out and clearly splitting up. Said they didn't want it. Great stuff too, a lot better than he could have afforded."

Kate was back and on her third Moet. I needed to ask about Joan and Jimmy before it was too late.

Her answer surprised me.

"She's a client of the office. I can't discuss her."

"Can you tell me anything? It does seem she might have run over my pal Jimmy, who you knew and liked."

"Jimmy I can discuss. Sweet guy, loved women and they loved him, but the partying and choice of dates finally caught up with him. He went broke before he could afford to party himself to death. I thought he was on the bright for a while recently, but seeing where he got run over — guess he'd fallen off the wagon, and hard."

Jimmy's maybe getting off the booze was news to me, but I was more interested in Joan. "Is there anything you can give me to help me understand Joan? I get mixed reviews."

She shook her head. "No, I have a great job, make good money, and have a great boss. I won't cross the line, even for you Tony."

That was that. I signed the bill, gave her a hug, and headed back to my place.

Maybe the body parts theory was it. Maybe Elsa was in on it, though it didn't seem so. There had to be another reason Kate was so negative on her — maybe a conflict with a guy? Maybe saw her in the same outfit at a party? May have just been some female thing we boys will never understand.

But I couldn't ignore it. As I'd found in the past, she was definitely wired into the town's goings on.

I called Frank and told him the body part story, which seemed to catch his attention. I was expecting some remark about me drinking with an ex, but it didn't come. He was so focused on Elsa, my romantic trivia was no longer a subject of fun.

Maybe Rebecca could help.

CHAPTER 18

Back at Plutocrats Paradise

Joe Gardino was watching the rear view mirror. It appeared they weren't being followed, which would be easy to spot. Davos isn't exactly a booming metropolis. The town really consists of a narrow valley couple of miles long with two main streets, a few dozen connecting side streets, and gorgeous mountains on either side.

At a little over 5,000 feet above sea level, Davos is the highest city in Europe. People with asthma or lung problems visit clinics for the clean air year round, while others ski in the winter. For five days in late January it's a meeting place for the world's most rich and powerful at the World Economic Forum.

But Joseph wasn't thinking about the clean air. He'd taken a photo of the men on the steps just after he broke their necks. He'd texted them to a "colleague" in Genoa who would send back a rundown on each. He hadn't wanted to seem concerned in front of Emily, but he was, and knew Gabriella was as well. She had made light of it with her: "any fool with a gun" remark, but both knew these men were dangerous and they may not have been alone. Either he had been lucky or they'd been, as Gabriella said, stupid. Their Armani Zoot suits were definitely not Davos vacation wear, and they were checking their weapons before climbing the stairs. It took Joseph, who was in a chair by the stairs pretending to read the morning paper, maybe 30 seconds for his powerful hands to snap necks and kill them both. Others may be less obvious and more difficult to spot, he thought.

He took an abrupt left into the half-full parking lot at the hotel Europe, pulled in facing the entrance and parked.

Emily looked up from her conversation to see what was happening, but Gabriella, knowing Joseph was just being cautious, patted her hand and smiled. *Will I ever meet this wonderful man?*

"Oh yes, I hope one day you will, and perhaps I will see your Anthony again as well." She let out a slow sigh. "Do you ever wish for a normal life?"

"Oh yes, that's my goal, and I am perhaps not that far from it."

Joseph, who got out of the car and walked toward the street with his cell phone, returned.

As they headed back to the hotel, he was checking a message. He smiled and held up two fingers, then clenched his fist — a signal to Gabriella that there were only two; the threat was over (for now).

CHAPTER 19

Rebecca at the Grill

I t had been a month or more since I last visited this place where I was once a regular.

It was about five-thirty. By six-thirty it would be an hour wait for dinner at the bar. The dining room wait at the Grill is ridiculous. You have to call on the 15th to get a reservation in the following month. I had parked in back and grabbed the first seat at the end of the bar, by the open kitchen area.

Rebecca, with her perfect smile, spotted me and came over. I have a CD that someone put together where she is featured on a few of the songs. She should have been featured on all of them, not that the others are bad; her voice is just that good.

"Hi stranger. Long time no see. What'll you have, the usual?"

She brought back a Dewar's and placed it on a napkin in front of me. "Sorry to hear that nice Mrs. Fisher died. Weren't you two friends?"

"I'd like to think we were. At least as close as a poor stiff from a tenement in Boston's North End can be with a woman 30 plus years older and a couple hundred million richer."

"Don't sell yourself short Tony. No one sees humanity more closely than a bartender at this place. I can guarantee money doesn't always bring happiness, and it sure don't bring class."

Having heard a few multimillionaires slaughter the English language, I smiled at the "don't."

A few people were coming in and taking seats near me at the bar. I figured I'd better get right to it. "Speaking of old money, what do you know about Joan Diamond?"

She smiled and held up a finger as if to say hold on a second, then asked the couple two seats away what they would like to drink and handed them a menu.

I could tell by her look she wanted to answer, or at the very least, discuss Joan.

Rebecca leaned forward on the bar and seemed to be telling me what I already knew. "She's a mystery." Then spotting another customer, she gave me the "I'll be right back" signal.

Finally, things settled down and the other bartender, realizing Rebecca wanted to talk, started taking orders.

"Tony, I personally like her. She is very cordial, polite to an extreme and has a great sense of humor, but..."

She paused and gave me that million-dollar smile. "Other brokers seem to love her or hate her. There is no — and I mean no — middle ground. Maybe jealousy, because she does real well, but it's weird."

Rebecca waved to a gentleman behind me to my right. "Don't turn or look now, Tony, but a gentleman friend of hers just came in. Interesting guy, a former neurosurgeon you know, operates on people's brains. She calls him Ben. I think he's retired, just consulting, lecturing, and writing papers on brain stuff. They don't seem involved romantically but they meet here at the bar often. I think he's been living in Wellington for several years and is considering moving to Palm Beach. He must have some money. She's shown him photos of major, like on the water serious, Palm Beach homes."

My ears perked up. Brain surgeon? Possibly experiments with zombies on drugs, far-fetched? Maybe not. Things were starting to connect.

"What else do they talk about? His work?"

"They spend a lot of time on really heavy stuff, how different parts of the brain function, what parts you can remove to solve physical problems, and some mind control stuff, like in the movies.

She seems to have a pretty good understanding of the subject as well."

She stopped, as though she had just remembered, "Oh, he has a slight accent, maybe Persian."

I nodded. "Wow I'm impressed. You can tell a Persian accent?"

She smiled, "Of course not, I heard him mention growing up in Persia."

I asked, "You know her background?"

She gave me that classic Rebecca smile, "You mean the Haitian nanny stuff? Could it all connect? Psychology and voodoo, don't know. What they discuss is way beyond that Sigmund Freud and Carl Jung's collective unconscious bit, I vaguely remember from college psychology."

She spotted a couple waiting for drinks. "Hey, gotta go. If you want an introduction let me know."

I shook my head. "Not now."

I left a twenty for the Dewar's but as I stood to leave, I realized I could see Joan's friend clearly in the mirror behind the bar. He was short, slim, dark-skinned, and quite handsome in a perfectly fitting tan Armani suit, very polished, and with a cleanly trimmed short white beard and mustache. Everything in place, I guess a good attribute for a guy who has to take your brain apart and put the pieces back in the right spot.

But what was his connection to Joan, let alone Jimmy, if any? I decided to hang around a bit, see if she showed up, and maybe get some more detail from Rebecca.

I sat back down, caught Rebecca's eye, and pointed to my glass. She came over and leaned into the bar.

"How's your love life, Tony?"

Before I could answer, she said, "See the two women at the far end of the bar?"

I had no recognition and I gave a, if you say so, shrug.

"The one on the left tried to pick you up in here about five years ago, remember? It was late. The place was thinning out. You were sitting, talking casually to a woman who was a stool away. That one came over and said to her, "He's a wasp and you're Jewish, he should be with me. I have a jeweler friend on Worth Avenue I can fix you up with."

I laughed, "How could I forget? She had a fight with her boyfriend, and he'd split. The nice woman I was talking to was, I'm sure, not interested in me, nor being fixed up with that nut-ball's jeweler friend."

I took a sip of my Dewar's and thought a minute.

"When I got outside, she was standing there, said her car was at Cucina, so I gave her a ride. We had a drink and she gave me her number. She said she couldn't tell me her real name because she came from a wealthy family and didn't want it to influence my decision about her, which, by the way, I'd already made."

"Well, I don't know if she has recognized you or not, she'd had a few that night, but her friend asked about you and, she is verrry good looking.

Rebecca is not prone to exaggerate so her emphasis on the very did tickle my interest.

The incognito Wasp and her attractive friend were at the opposite end where the bar turns to face back my way. She looked great from a distance, but in a town where Botox is as common as eye shadow, coupled with something in the air that causes some women's breasts to mature late, like in their mid-thirty's, it's best to get a closer look.

"May I buy them a drink?"

"I'll ask."

I had planned to head home and relax, watch a little TV, maybe talk with Elsa after she met with the ex-CIA spy and her sister.

Rebecca was back. "They said they'd love a drink, but only if you'd come over and join them."

Why not a quick visit with an attractive woman, I thought. It seems impolite to not at least say hello.

She smiled and said, "Looks like they may only be here for drinks. I'll have people needing those seats for dinner. I'd prefer they take the high top behind them anyway."

I had already convinced myself their end of the bar was a better position to watch Joan's friend, and hopefully Joan.

I stood up and whispered to Rebecca. "The hardship I endure for you."

"All right, Tony, no tears."

I headed through the still thin crowd to their end of the bar. "You ladies would probably feel less crowded and more comfortable at the high top behind you. Would you care to join me?"

I sat with my back to the wall next to Rebecca's Miss Very Attractive, who turned out to be a Mrs., in the legal process of becoming a Miss, and across from the woman who called me a Wasp to the very nice Jewish woman, who I didn't really know, when she had tried to swap me for her jeweler friend on Worth Avenue.

If that makes any sense, you'll fit right in here in Palm Beach.

Fortunately, she didn't recognize me. Plus, Mrs. Attractive, who went by Eva, was not just good looking, but very funny. She was a mild cross between Ingrid Bergman and Joan Rivers, but without the Rivers laugh. She was above average height and slim. She was wearing a very low cut blue dress that matched her eyes and contained a serious chest that appeared homegrown. Her wide smile created a slight wrinkle beside her very deep blue eyes. It gave the impression she was winking at you. She explained her country of origin: she was conceived in Norway and born in Brooklyn.

I ordered a few appetizers of fried oysters, jumbo shrimp and two artichokes, most women's favorites. Soon, I was enjoying the best combination of looks and personality I'd experienced in a while.

I consider myself a pretty good storyteller, but she caught my attention when she enhanced her stories by easily switching from one accent to another.

Normally women, and I'm sure we men as well, become better or worse looking after you get to know them. Another transformation with an exceptionally attractive woman who is fun, smart and interesting is you forget it was looks that got you over there. Sex temporarily takes a back seat, and often, unless the woman makes the move, it doesn't happen. Next time you meet, or even several meetings later, a touch or just a hint of her perfume can ignite memories of the initial physical desire, which, having been pushed below the surface has grown even stronger. Now it's more complicated; she's become a friend.

We had finished two drinks and the appetizers. Eva was halfway through a story about her wealthy ex-husband, who she had chosen to leave and forego alimony, when I saw Rebecca waving from the bar.

I was interested in the no alimony bit. I had met several very attractive women over the years that had left wealthy and powerful men, but been so anxious to get out that they accepted no alimony, no money at all — nothing but the children, which in most cases the ex-husband eventually lured back with money anyway.

Rebecca was pointing to the bearded neurosurgeon and whom I guessed from the back was Joan Diamond. It appeared they had paid their check and were about to leave by the back door.

I was in a fix, which fortunately Rebecca, who was occasionally checking on my progress, picked up on. She leaned over the bar holding her fist by her ear as though I had a call and waved for me to come over.

I excused myself and walked the few step to the bar.

"They are just leaving, Tony. Their conversation got a little heated, like there is a problem. The surgeon, Ben, had stepped away from the bar toward the door, seemed to be returning a call. When he came back, even though they only half-finished their meal, they asked for the check. "

I handed her a credit card. "I'll tell the ladies I have an emergency, that a friend is ill; I need to go to the Good Sam."

"No problem." She gave me her biggest smile, and said, "And Tony, thank you so much for taking the ladies to the high top." She patted the back of my hand resting on the bar. "That Norwegian woman looks like tough duty, and you did it all for me."

Turning back to the table I said, "Eva, what is your favorite ice cream?"

She came right back with, "Was your call from an ice cream parlor? You certainly have interesting contacts, Mr. Tauck, but to answer your question, my current favorite is chocolate, but how did they know we had just finished our meal?"

"No, a friend is in trouble, I have to go." I took her hand. "When was the last time you were asked on a date for an ice cream?"

"George Harrington, 8th grade." She pretended a blush. "Cutest boy in the class."

"I was wondering if we might put off desert until tomorrow afternoon at Sprinkles, best ice cream in Florida, maybe anywhere."

She smiled and gave my hand a squeeze. "If we can meet right at noon it would be perfect for me. I have to meet a friend early afternoon."

As I headed toward the back door, Rebecca waved me over again. "Tony, maybe it's my imagination, but I thought I saw a hint of recognition between your new friend and Joan."

I was sorry I hadn't known it earlier, but recognition could mean they were best friends or had met casually at a benefit.

Maybe we'll have time to discuss it over ice cream.

CHAPTER 20

The Chase

Joan's red Jaguar convertible was just backing out and heading across the mall parking lot toward Cocoanut Row side, which runs north and south parallel to the lake.

I jumped in my Mercedes, waited for them to put a little distance between us, and then followed slowly with my lights out.

They took a hard left to cut down alongside the sister building south of the Grill.

I figured if they headed out this side they'd go south on Cocoanut. I drove to the far right side of the lot past a beautiful old Banyan tree and came out about fifty yards south, where I figured they'd pass. If they saw my car, I would appear to have come from McCarthy's, not the Grill.

I lucked out; about a minute later Joan's red Jag passed, heading south in a hurry.

I switched mental gears from the divorcing Norwegian to the brain guy's getting a call so important that Joan would leave her artichoke unfinished, if, in fact, that was the order in which it occurred.

It wasn't clear if they argued, then he made a call, or the call caused the friction. Maybe she was pushing him for something and he finally agreed, but had to call first. Or possibly there was an emergency somewhere they had to tend to.

I didn't have a long checklist of where they might be headed. My only question was where they warehoused the bodies, not much else.

Traffic was thin; I waited to get one car between us and pulled out.

I checked my watch. Twenty past eight. The North Bridge, also named the Flagler, is on the quarter of, quarter past schedule. I still had that Mecca property in my mind and was wondering if they might still go north. Were they only heading south to the middle bridge because of the North Bridge traffic backup?

A couple hundred yards down the road, I passed the 75 rooms, 100,000 square-foot Gilded Age mansion, Whitehall. Henry Flagler had built as a wedding present for what we now refer to as a "trophy wife," Mary Lily Kenan Flagler. The couple used the home as a winter retreat from 1902 until Flagler's death in 1913, establishing the Palm Beach season for the super wealthy of the Gilded Age.

Apparently nothing has changed much in politics. When Flagler wanted to divorce his first wife to marry Mary Lily, he had the legislature change the law, making insanity a reason for divorce.

The car just ahead was slower than I had hoped. Joan's Jaguar was probably one hundred yards ahead and the gap was growing. It would be just my luck for them to hit the bridge, make it across, and I'd catch the on-the-hour- half-hour bridge closing. The road is narrow with two blind turns, tough to pass until after the second curve, leaving only about 300 yards of narrow straight away before the right onto Royal Palm and across the bridge.

I inched up close to the guy in front of me, wanting to pass but not wanting to be noticed.

It didn't matter. Joan hit the light on the corner at yellow, and to my surprise, sailed straight through the intersection staying south on Cocoanut.

I sat at the red light watching her Jag get smaller and smaller as it sped past Brazilian, Australian, Chilean, and out of sight. When the light finally turned, I stepped on the gas, got up to Australian and thought I'd lost her. I'd been able to watch her for a couple of blocks, so knew she got at least as far as Chilean, but that's one-way heading west to the inter-coastal. Seeing nothing, I took the next left on Peruvian and drove rapidly east toward South County.

I glanced left as I passed the parking lot just after the Preservation Society. There they were, toward the rear of the lot, just getting out of her car. I continued past about one hundred yards and sat on the opposite side watching for them to come out, to hopefully see where they were going.

I sat and waited for probably twenty minutes. When they didn't reappear, I got out and walked cautiously back on the opposite side of the street to check out the lot where they had parked. From where I was standing, the lot was shaped like an upside down L, narrow at the street end and opening to the right behind three buildings. There was an office on the street with two buildings behind it. The lot was clearly closed for the night with just a few scattered cars.

I walked cautiously across the street then, hugging the side of the office in front, crept past the second building, and hearing a TV on the first floor, I deduced it to be apartments. They had parked beyond the three buildings, but within view of the street. They had to be in the rear building.

I inched my way around the last building, a square white concrete two-story structure with a loading dock at the rear.

I climbed the four worn wooden steps to the platform and tried to gently open the sliding door. It was closed tight. There was no light coming from the building that appeared to have no windows.

I stood with my ear to the door, trying to pick up on any voices — until I felt the door start to open.

I leaped off the platform and raced to the street, hoping not to be seen. Huddled by the side of the real estate office, peeking around the corner, I watched Joan and the brain surgeon walking slowly to her car. They were talking intensely about something.

I was about to head to my car to follow them when a third person came down the steps, waved to them and got in a beat up old Ford flatbed.

I was sure of it. Tall, lean, long arms, unkempt hair — it was the guy from the lab — Adam, who had asked Elsa about us.

I had Kate telling me Elsa was not on the up and up, and this geek was her friend, lover, whatever. Was she in on this deal?

I got to my car and sat. Whatever it was that caused the issue at the Grill seemed settled. I started my engine and sat a minute until they cleared the area, then drove back to the Grill.

I was curious to know what the neurosurgeon was driving. It seemed unlikely there was anything more than a business arrangement between these two, but I wanted to be sure.

He drove off in a brand new steel gray Lexus LS 600. Joan sat for a minute and then headed off in a different direction.

My guess seemed right. He wasn't her type, or perhaps she was not his?

Just in case you're wondering, I did peek my head in the door of the Grill, but no luck. I'll have to settle for an ice cream lunch at Sprinkles.

I sat for a minute wondering what could be in that building in the middle of Palm Beach — zombies, body parts, who knows what. Then I remembered Vinnie Carangelo's comment on Haitian beliefs. They must remain in contact with the deceased. Was Jimmy in the building, and Joan needing to make regular contact?

My sense was they had locked up for the night and left. It was cool and overcast. The parking lot by the building had been empty. Maybe I could get a closer look.

I drove back, parked on the side street between two other cars, and opened my glove compartment. I took out a small case with five picks that will open most locks. The street was deserted. I sprinted across the street, around the corner, along the side of what seemed like a real estate office, and past the window where I had heard the TV.

It was pretty dark, the lights and TV were off. I walked quickly to the rear of the building and climbed the short set of steps to the platform.

I had to hand it to them. If this is where the bodies were stored, right here in the heart of Palm Beach, a block from Worth Avenue and, God forbid, the Everglades Club, this sure wouldn't have been anyone's first guess.

The pen light on my key ring was bright enough for what I needed to accomplish. The sliding door had a simple wafer lock where you just need to separate the two sets of pins so the cylinder will turn. A couple minutes later, I was in.

It was pitch dark and deadly silent. My penlight was no match for the darkness and size of the space, but it did the job short range for what I needed.

I felt my way along, beside what seemed to be a large laboratory counter with various types of computerized equipment.

I was picturing a Dr. Frankenstein and a body hooked up to all kinds of wires and gauges breathing life into it, when suddenly, a light went on at the far end of the building.

I ducked down, turned my pen light off, and scooted on my hands and knees to the door I had just entered. I stopped at the door and listened. Apparently I hadn't been noticed. There was no voice coming from the light at the far end, only the faint sound of foot-steps. Maybe a night watchman getting up to use the bathroom?

Interesting, I thought. Seems he was locked in for the night.

Judging from the size of the building, there could easily be re-frigerated boxes similar to the morgue at the watchman's end, but it appeared unlikely I could do much without his knowing I was there.

Time to split.

On the way back to my place, I called Frank. "Give me a run-down on Elsa's meeting with the Clematis Street spy," then paused as though I were hanging up before continuing, "Followed Joan to what may be the place where they keep the bodies."

Waiting for a return call, I watched a little TV, the end of a 1940s film with a coincidentally current theme: Double Indemnity. The plot is about an insurance salesman who has an illicit affair with the seductive wife of his client, and then helps her kill the husband for his insurance.

As I watched the credits I checked my cell. No call from Frank.

CHAPTER 21

The Other Rebecca

I got up early and finally made it to Ultima Fitness to work out; subsequently, I was given a scolding by my friend Dyane in the form of pretending she didn't remember me.

I was back at my place just getting out of the shower when Frank called.

"What's this warehouse in the middle of Palm Beach business?"

I wasn't sure if I should introduce the subject of Elsa's morgue mate, Adam. He'd had a pretty negative play yesterday from Kate.

Better to leave that one alone, at least until I could check it out some other way. Plus, I knew if I told Frank I'd seen him leave the building with Joan and the neurosurgeon, for sure, he'd tell Elsa. And what if she were involved?

Whether or not Adam was Elsa's former or current lover, they had a history. It had never been clear to me whether her motives were directed at solving the mystery of her husband's death or what was going on with Joan. For sure, if I told Frank in his lovesick state, he'd tell her.

I filled him in on my visit to the Grill, Joan's friend Ben, and my return trip to the building on Peruvian.

He was quiet for a moment, and then said, "I met Elsa after her meeting with Rebecca and her sister Stacey. As soon as Elsa told them of her husband's career and death, they both really opened up.

Stacey had a best friend who was forced to resign for strictly political reasons and is still pretty sore about it. She is still involved in what she calls 'projects,' most of which are handled on a 'need to know' basis, but has friends that are full time. Plus, there are rumors that a rogue group, backed by some country that doesn't like us, may be experimenting with creating human drones, you know, manipulating their brains and actions from a distance. They are working on a way to program some percentage of the hundred billions of neurons that make up the brain, to make the subject follow orders sent by a device the size of a cell phone."

I interrupted, "There has been a lot of press on brain research lately. Mort Zuckerman just donated two hundred million for brain research — of course for a slightly different purpose than the building on Peruvian. Who knows where else these little labs are, but why would they be doing the developing here, and not in their own country?"

Frank replied, "She's not intimately involved, not up to date, but did say that if they are set up here in the states they may have advanced way beyond where we thought this field has gone. Think about it, Tony, they use people as experiments, while in this country we are still using mice and worms. The first group that understands the brain in a way to be able to manipulate actions — program people to do as the programmer chooses — has a major advantage."

I understood where he was going with this but had to add, "Why Palm Beach of all the places they could be?"

"I don't know, Tony, other than if I interpolate from what Stacey said, it's probably not the only place they're doing it."

I wasn't going to risk it but decided to at least raise the subject. "What did Elsa think of this Stacey, is she believable?"

"Yes, very sound, didn't seem to exaggerate, weighed her words carefully; clearly well trained."

"Did she get any feedback from her friend in the lab on other bodies going out?"

"She asked, and he kind of brushed it off, said he must have been mistaken, Joan and Jimmy were the only situation he was sure of."

"I don't know Frankie; this might just be beyond my pay grade. Do you think we should involve the feds? Maybe Perez has a contact we can trust."

Frank hadn't replied so I continued, "Course we really don't have much to go on. We think Joan is involved in some scam for insurance on Jimmy, and who knows what else. But every time I bring up her name to an attorney, he can't comment because she's a client. Your pal Ralph shut up like a clam when we raised the issue of Jimmy, and that was before we even knew about Joan. Now we have a building on Peruvian with something that looks like lab equipment. Not enough to get a CIA swat team out here in a hurry."

Frank was chuckling. "You're right, we need to find Jim's body, and the best bet is the building you visited last night. If zombies, or whatever, are in there, we need to find a way in."

I was nodding, pleased we were in agreement. "I guess we can park down the street and watch, hopefully find when only one watchman is there, and see if there's a way to distract him."

I checked my watch. It was only eight o'clock. "I'll go now for a few hours, if you can take over at about eleven thirty. I have to be somewhere at noon."

Pre-Elsa, I'd have gotten riddled with sarcasm and questions. Now that Frank was in love, I got a simple, "Who you meeting?"

My reply: "Nice woman I met at the Grill, taking her for an ice cream, just getting acquainted," was enough.

CHAPTER 22

The Stakeout

The entrance to the lot is on Peruvian, but it stretches a full block to Chilean with Hibiscus running up the west side. Hibiscus, with only a short hedge and a few thin trees, allowed me a closer look at the door and loading dock. But unlike the other streets, it's a little too narrow to park for three hours and not be obvious.

I decided on Chilean, which is one way going west, not as obvious as Peruvian, plus the bush is a little thicker and the street is plenty wide, with cars on the parking lot side. I was perhaps 50 yards from the back loading dock, which in daylight still seemed the only way in and out.

I sat for a while with my binoculars on the door and then got out and walked down Hibiscus and back to stretch my legs. Finally, I got back in the car and just sat.

I wondered about Jimmy. Is he dead, alive, was he even in there? On the surface the most outgoing, fun guy you could meet, but tough to know what was going on inside. He seemed to live day-to-day without a care, as though there was no future. He was always pursuing some dream, the perfect woman, or just the next best day of his life.

Had life's realities finally caught up with him? Was Joan the villain? Perhaps, but if not her, then it would be someone else. It had just been a matter of time. There had been a long string of Joan's loving his humor, his love of fun. But his feelings, too exposed, too close to the surface, required an excess of passion in return. When unfulfilled, only a new woman could quiet the excess.

Was this living each day, belief in no future, also a fear of death? On top of AA, had Jimmy also attended funerals? Is that how he and Joan had met? Was he a volunteer in this zombie experiment and not really the down and out derelict more recently portrayed?

A tap on the window interrupted my reverie.

It was Frank. "I tried your cell. No answer. I've been driving around the block looking for your car and finally spotted you here in the bushes. Its quarter to twelve. Don't you have a...," he hesitated and winked, "business meeting at noon?" I checked my cell. It read ten to twelve and there was a message. "Looks like I had the sound off on the cell. No one in or out since I've been here. Right, I'm late, better get going."

CHAPTER 23

Ice Cream and More

As I headed north on Cocoanut, retracing the routes that lead me to this so-called zombie building the night before, I checked my messages.

There was one from my friend Dorothy Sullivan, asking if I'd like to attend a fundraiser for kids. She's been the heart and soul of the less publicized side of Palm Beach Charities, those for local causes. As rich as the town is, the short distance across the bridge to the real Florida reveals, in spots, the same problems of poverty, poorly funded schools, and abuse found in any major city.

Dorothy with her husband John, who recently passed away, has been championing their causes with charity balls at The Breakers and Mar-A-Lago for decades.

The second call got my juices flowing.

Hello Tony, thank you for dinner and a very entertaining evening. With my troublesome divorce, it's been awhile since I felt this comfortable with a man. Look forward to licking a cone with you."

There was a slight hesitation, and then she closed with, "Is your home close by? I would enjoy seeing where this sexy man lives."

I stepped on the gas, headed across Royal Poinciana, and parked around the corner from Sprinkles.

I got out of the car, paid the meter, stood for a minute, and took a deep breath.

It's not like I've never had a date, although it's been awhile since it was for ice cream. But by asking to see my place, she had removed a step in the seduction process. Don't get me wrong. I was excited. A gorgeous, fun, and interesting woman throws out the word sexy and wants to go to my place after ice cream? It's just that the normal process of pursuit was out of place.

I'm a decent looking guy, but this was, like, way too easy.

Maybe her friend at the Grill who gave me her number that I never called actually did recognize me.

Was it a set up?

Hell, I thought, don't look a gift horse in the mouth.

I stepped to the front, around the potted ferns to see Eva sitting outside in one of the metal green 1950s lawn chairs. She was talking to a woman in the next chair.

Were they together? All of a sudden too easy went to the back burner. Maybe this is—just for ice cream.

Her skirt was light blue, knee length, and loose fitting, not exactly matching the message on my cell. But she did have on heels and black nylons, causing me to wonder if they were panty hose or held up by a garter belt. I prefer thinking about the possibilities of a garter belt and started to picture her with a leg up on a chair, knee bent, leaning down to unsnap the garters one by one in that loose fitting halter top. I was a little unsure of whether she was purposely giving off mixed messages or if my over thinking was confusing what should be a simple process.

One thing was for sure. That is a good-looking woman.

She waved from her chair, then stood and gave me a hug that lasted awhile.

Though she had been in the shade, it was a warm day and I could feel the heat from her soft full breasts against my cotton shirt.

She turned to her friend. "Ingrid, say hello to Tony." I bent down and took the hand of an older woman, tanned, and well outfitted in a purple velvet dress and matching feathered hat that reminded me of Jimmy's story about working on Worth Avenue.

"We just met, and found we have much in common, but I have her card."

She linked her arm in mine and squeezed my hand. "Come inside and buy me that ice cream you promised."

Just inside, Eva exclaimed excitedly, "Oh this is so much fun. Look at these photos of visitors to this nice ice cream parlor: John Lennon, Glenn Beck, Tony Robbins with his family…"

She gave me a wink. "Smart woman putting Beck and Lennon on opposite walls."

I pointed to another photo. "Here's Donna, the owner, with Bob Kraft, who owns a successful little place himself."

We took our cones from the two attractive girls at the counter: Hanna and Shannon, grabbed a stack of napkins, and moved to the white leather couch under a copy of Town and Country magazine's article listing Sprinkles as one of the three best ice cream parlors in the country.

I pointed to her triple chocolate. "You know Elsa, the original name of that flavor was Better than Sex. I think Donna changed the name because too many kids were asking their parents too many questions."

She stood up from the couch and leaned over me. "Have a lick. I may quiz you later on whether it is."

Then, still standing over me, she read the article in People Magazine. "Look Tony, my flavor, Triple Chocolate… I mean, Better than Sex is rated tops in the country." She sat back down, this time closer so our thighs and shoulders almost touched.

"This reminds me of my first date," she said as she quickly slid closer. "I was taken for ice cream by that cute George Harrington; he didn't sit close, either. I had to move over then, too. What is it with you men? Can't you tell when a girl is interested? Besides, sharing a cone is about as close to kissing as you can get without actually kissing."

The woman was clearly getting my interest.

"How did things eventually work out between you and George?"

"He walked me home with his arm around my waist, and then we stood against a tree in my backyard kissing and rubbing up against each other — what we kids called dry humping. When he left he had a big wet spot in the front of his khaki pants."

She leaned over and looked up at me while she licked my cone. "George didn't know it, but my panties were plenty wet too."

"Did you dry hump on your first date, Tony? Fun isn't it?"

Actually I had, but wasn't sure whether I was getting aroused by her story or the memory of my first. Regardless, she sure knew how to press a guy's buttons.

Not wanting to interrupt her seduction, I nodded and offered her another taste of my butter-crunch cone. She bent over and licked while looking up at me and smiling. "I love to lick."

I stood and held out my hand, "You said you wanted to see my place. My car is right here, and I live barely two blocks away."

As she stood up from the couch, she leaned forward to reveal those soft warm breasts I had felt through her shirt only a few minutes before. My mind was churning with possibilities. Would I start there and work my way down, or start with her firm inner thighs and work up?

As you might have guessed, she didn't wait for me to decide.

Before we had walked the twenty yards to the car, she had her arms around my neck pulling me close, pushing her thighs against mine and kissing my lips softly, like she probably had done to young George. It took every bit of will power I could muster to not respond as he had.

I opened the car to let her slide in, and then around to the driver side, hoping no one I knew was watching.

I started the car and before I had even pulled out into the light traffic she was running her fingers slowly up my right thigh and trying to loosen my belt. I took a right on Sunrise, then in the interest of safety I pulled her hand away from my thigh while I drove the block and a half to my place, and put her fingers in my mouth for safe keeping.

Fortunately we were alone in the parking lot when she got out of the car. This time her tongue touched my lips lightly then explored my mouth as I walked her backward the ten steps to my door. Freeing one hand to open the door, I picked her up, carried her in, and deposited her onto my queen-size unmade bed.

Before I could join her, she stood up quickly, kicked off her shoes, unzipped and dropped her skirt, leaving what she would do with the black nylons to my imagination. I went to the bureau, slipped in a CD, then moved onto the bed where she was patting the sheet next to her.

I was a little taken back by what appeared to be her putting on the brakes.

I stood still for a few seconds while she propped herself comfortably on a pillow and said, "I love foreplay. Do you mind if I tell you a story?"

I'm sure my big grin gave her the answer she wanted, but I answered anyway.

"Anything worth doing is worth doing well," I let my pants drop to the floor, joined her on the bed and lay quietly on my back wondering what was next: the handcuffs, the blindfold, or what?

Instead, she rolled over on her left side so her breasts, held in by only a soft silk halter-top, leaned warmly against my chest.

Just then, the music started.

"Oh my goodness, I was expecting the usual Frank Sinatra, but Pachelbel's Canon," she said, laughing. "This is Palm Beach class."

She kissed me softly on the cheek and neck, and then took my left hand and placed it on her right breast, allowing me to feel her now extended nipple through the soft silk of her halter-top and said again, "May I tell you a story?"

To which I, of course, nodded my approval.

She began. "I had my first really great sex a few days before my 17th birthday. Peter was an older man; he was Greek, a neighbor, maybe 35 or 36, worked at home as a writer on short stories for magazines. He was divorced with two young girls who visited with him every other weekend. He was not overly handsome, but I had often watched him from my bedroom window sunbathing in his backyard. He was very muscular, very masculine."

She was running her fingers in big circles over my chest and stomach, occasionally sticking her tongue in my ear as she continued in a warm whisper.

"I know it sounds terrible, young girl seduced by older man. But really, I seduced him. I was definitely not a virgin, but aware enough to know what I was getting from boys my age was not real sex. I wanted the real thing, real bad."

"I had known him, had a young girl's crush when he was still married, his girls just babies. That was long before I had breasts or any shape at all. In those days I could sit on his lap or give him a young girl's hug and it was all innocent fun. But as I slowly became a woman, my feelings became sexual. He sensed it and pulled away."

She reached down and with just her fingertips was slowly stoking me through my jockey shorts. "I had a photograph of him in a tight bathing suit I had taken from his house; I fantasized about what he would be like and masturbated while looking at his picture. I knew his schedule: when he went to the gym, when he had girlfriends over — and there were plenty. Seemed like every woman but the Lone Ranger's daughter.

When his daughters visited I made a point of being out in the yard to meet them, welcome them, and help them carry their things into his house. I even volunteered to babysit if he had to run out when they were there.

"One day I had just left the bags in his daughter's room and realized I was alone. I opened the door to his bedroom, which was just across the hall. The second floor had high cathedral ceilings and his bed was as large as I had ever seen. I quietly crept over and lay spread eagled in the center of his bed touching myself and fantasizing that he was lying beside me.

My daydream was broken by his voice calling me from down stairs. I slid off the bed and headed for the door. As I left the room I took one more sweeping gaze and looked up. There, hanging from a beam were two ropes, like a swing. In my inexperienced state I wondered, why a swing in his bedroom, then forgot about it.

I raced downstairs and out the door, half embarrassed by almost being caught in his bedroom, and half being so turned on by my little fantasy that I couldn't have made much sense anyway.

I stayed away for a while hoping he would miss me, but he hadn't seemed to, so I went back to showing up when he was with his girls, dressed in my tight shorts and sweaters. Finally, I knew I was getting to him. When I ran into him, he seemed to avoid stopping to talk. He seemed more in a hurry, which, as you might imagine, just strengthened my resolve."

I lay there thinking, I don't have Emile's desire for women half his age, but seeing what she looked and felt like now, and imagining her as a younger, even firmer version, was getting me more than a little turned on.

Of course, her slowly stroking me through the soft cotton in my shorts didn't hurt, either.

Able to easily judge my increasing level of interest with her hand in my shorts, she removed her hand and slowly took off her halter-top. She then placed my hand back on her nipple and slowly rolled closer, her warm breath and soft lips still whispering in my ear.

"I remember every detail of this day, and maybe two or three times a year still masturbate while daydreaming about it."

While pronouncing the word "masturbate," she gave me a gentle squeeze.

"On this particular day, Peter was out in the yard by his pool, in his lounge chair writing. I opened the gate and walked over, asked if I could join him. He smiled, pointed to the chair next to his, and kept writing. I stood directly in his line of sight and slowly loosened my skirt; taking my time as though I was having trouble getting it unfastened, then, finally let it drop to the grass, revealing the very skimpiest bikini bottom I could buy. I have been told I have a nice body now, what is thirty years later, so believe me, at 17, I was tight."

I looked down at her nearly perfect breasts and flat stomach, at her probable current age of 46, and smiled.

She continued, "Next I did the same routine with my blouse. I unbuttoned just enough to reveal the bikini top, which was purposely too small for my breasts, then slowly leaned down to pick up the skirt, walked it over my lounge chair, then finished taking off my blouse."

About halfway through her story, which was turning both of us on, perhaps her even more than me if that was possible, she slowly moved my hand from her nipple, giving me a moment to hold her full breast in my hand before slowly running my fingertips down onto her stomach into her silk bikini underpants. She left my hand there for a long minute, then slipped the tip of my middle finger into her wet vagina and began moving it gently in a circular motion against her clit, which was firm, like a tiny erection.

Almost as though she had put her finger in a light socket, her body stiffened, her back arched and she gasped as though she had lost her breath. She held my hand there as to assure me it was the perfect spot.

She was silent for a moment and then clearly just getting started, she softly kissed my cheek and then my neck, and with my middle finger still resting on her spot, she continued her story of first sex, as a warm whisper in my ear.

"With my shirt off and now nearly naked but for my very small bikini, I stood in front of him and appeared to fumble in my bag, as though I was trying to find something. At this point, he was only pretending to be engrossed in his writing and was looking over his notepad to watch as I took out a bottle of baby oil. I poured a small amount from the bottle and spread a little on my arms and shoulders, then sat the bottle on its side at the foot of my lounge chair and said, 'I like to let it warm in the sun before I put it on. Only takes a few minutes to warm up. I hope you'll help me with the places I can't reach Peter.' I gave him my best smile and lay down on the lounge next to his."

Eva, who now had my shaft out and in her hand and was slowly running two fingers up the front, around the head, and back down with the lightest touch, whispered, "You don't happen to have any baby oil, do you Tony?"

I laughed. "Yes, but I'd rather not interrupt what you're doing."

"Hold on," she said, and reached into her purse on the table by the bed and pulled out a bottle with a Chinese symbol on the front. She poured a small amount into the hand that was stroking me. After a minute she leaned down so her lips were almost touching me then blew softly on the oil creating the most incredible warmth. I don't know what that little Chinese bottle was, but it sure felt good. It was almost as though I was already inside her.

I wanted to kiss her, actually a lot more, but she was breathing so heavily I could tell that she was getting as turned on by telling the story as I was by feeling it whispered in my ear. Plus, to be honest, the stroking wasn't half bad.

I waited, enjoying each second as she continued. "After what I hoped Peter thought was an eternity, and I did as well, I stood again, felt the bottle to confirm it was warm, and began slowly rubbing the warm oil first in my lower legs, then up and around my inner thighs next to my bikini. I let some drip on my chest and run down between my breasts to my stomach and into my bikini bottom. 'Oh that warm oil feels so good on my hot skin.' I said, then leaned over and reached down so my breasts were almost in his face and put some on his arm and shoulder.

I laid down on my stomach on the other lounge, loosened the string on my bikini top and said, 'Will you do my back Peter, please.'"

"My eyes were closed in anticipation. I could hear him stand, felt his weight on the lower part of the lounge as he knelt between my legs. I waited, then finally felt a line of oil drip up first my right thigh onto my back, then my left. His hands were large and sure as he smoothed the oil slowly up my thighs, his thumbs just brushing the edge of my string bikini He hesitated for a second as though he was holding my butt in his hands, then slowly moved up my back with his thumbs almost meeting in the center, allowing his two outside fingers to wrap around to the front. Feeling his hands coming, I lifted my head and shoulders so his fingers would brush my breasts. I couldn't see them, but knew my nipples were hard as a rock. Again, he ran the oil up my thigh and followed with his big hands reaching around me, this time massaging my nipples gently on their way by. I was so close to an orgasm; I desperately wanted to rollover on my back and take him inside me, but his hands held me in position.

'Feel good,' he asked. 'Yes, please don't stop,' I panted. 'Do it again, please.' This time he started to move his hands slowly up my legs, and then, reaching my knees, he picked up both legs and spread them wider so when his thumbs reached my bikini they gently touched me and I started to come. I was so hot I just wanted him inside me, his thumbs, his fingers, anything, but instead his hands moved slowly over my butt then thankfully, instead of continuing he dropped his thumbs, pushed my bikini aside and entered me with his right thumb. I screamed out at the pure pleasure. My body was shaking as he worked his thumb slowly back and forth. I had experienced sex with boys my own age, but they were always in a hurry. Not this time. He pulled his hands away and I started to move after them. 'Stay still,' he whispered. He pulled me up on my knees, and kneeling close behind me, he slid just the head of his cock into me. I was trying desperately to push toward him, to take him inside, but he had his arms firmly around me with his hands on my breasts so I couldn't move, couldn't get more of him inside me.

I pushed and pleaded, desperate for more. Finally, he thrust his full length into me from behind, causing the most excruciating combination of pleasure and pain imaginable. I had already had one incredible orgasm that seemed to last and last, but must have had four more before he finally collapsed on top of me."

Eva, now naked lying next to me, moved her head and mouth slowly down my chest and stomach, and this time took me in her mouth as though she wanted to swallow the entire length. The added feeling of her warm breasts on my thighs doubled the pleasure as she gently licked and fondled me as though imagining I was that first real lover. Finally she sat up, took a rubber ring and slid it down over my penis and whispered, "To keep you from coming too soon," then she rolled over on her hands and knees inviting me in.

Some women like sex, some women love sex, and if there were a next category she'd have made it. Each time I thrust into her she tightened up as if to hold me there, and then released me. It wasn't more than a few minutes before she started to moan and I could feel her orgasm engulfing me with her wetness. This went on and on, tightening then releasing through what seemed like either many or one very long orgasm. Her hands were gripping the headboard so hard her knuckles were white, but she kept going, pumping and squeezing.

To avoid a climax, I was trying to think of anything but what I was doing. Finally she somehow sensed I was ready and pushed me off. Then she rolled on her back, grabbed me, placed my cock between her breasts and took the full blast in her face and mouth, then wiped and licked what had missed her mouth, and swallowed.

"Protein, best vitamin there is," she laughed.

"Have to say Eva; you're definitely not a spitter."

She laid back and laughed, a rich hearty laugh, like she probably hadn't in a while, and then said, "Tony, all kidding aside, there are sperm cookbooks. It adds both an interesting taste and conversation to a meal with friends."

She laughed again. "Of course we usually tell them after they've eaten."

Thinking about her control over her body during sex, I said, "You must work out hours a day to be so toned."

"Oh, you mean the kegels," she smiled. "Yes, every day. I learned that trick from Peter. After that first seduction, we carried on for nearly three years in that high ceiling bedroom where I learned the joys of sex on a swing. He taught me about the wonderful world of pure pleasure. It was a lifelong gift."

We lay there talking for a bit. Then I glanced at my cell. I had put it on mute.

Frank had made four calls, and finally left a text. "Where the f--- are you?"

She leaned over, pressing her glorious breasts against my chest, and kissed me softly on the mouth.

Not normally a guy who sticks around for more than a polite period after casual sex, the softness of her breasts and lips started me wondering if she had a few more stories to share before I called Frank?

Instead of a story, I got a surprise.

She stood and slipped into her skirt, not needing to look for her bikini underwear, which had only been pushed aside.

I stood and held her close. "I'd forgotten how much I enjoyed those sugar cones. We must do it again."

Still close she whispered, "No, you are a beautiful charming man, but I need more. My looks and body won't last forever and I have found a fine man who is considerably older and extremely wealthy. We will marry in a week back in Michigan. I'm in Palm Beach with old friends as a last hurrah. My husband-to-be is a follower of the Latter Day Saints and believes sex is to procreate only."

She pulled away with a laugh. "He considers the missionary position kinky. But that is the tradeoff us women, and some men, are forced to make. But as you know, it is not a King Solomon choice. Sex is momentary, and as the yearnings fade with age, the desire for sex dims. The little girl in us also gets pleasure by being dressed in designer gowns and photographed at fancy parties and openings."

She was quiet on the drive back.

As I parked behind her car, she reached into her pocketbook, and with a big smile, pulled out a pair of handcuffs.

She was laughing as she dangled them in front of me. "I had these just in case my story of first sex didn't keep you still. Fun not needing them."

I got out and opened her door. She stepped out and formally extended her hand. "Thank you Tony. That was a fitting sendoff to my new life."

I stood quietly next to my car as she drove off.

A wise woman, I thought.

CHAPTER 24

Distraction at the Lab

I knew I had taken a lot longer than it should to buy a girl an ice cream, but Frank's text seemed a little harsh. Figure I'd better listen to his messages.

At 12:26, he said, "Tony, get back here quick, I have to move my car. I'm blocking someone's space."

Then, at 12:56: "Tony, I went to move my car, got a couple blocks away and a guy in uniform waved me over to the side of the road; said there'd been an accident. Pointed me to park in close behind an old truck. I sat there for a while, and then noticed the cop had walked off. Just as I decided to leave and head back, the car behind me pulled in close almost touching my bumper. The driver got out and ran; the cop had disappeared. I'm stuck between the car and the truck. Looks like a set up to get me away from the building. Where are you?"

Just about when Eva was in the middle of her baby oil story, I thought.

Was I set up too? Rebecca had said she thought Eva and Joan had exchanged looks. Pretty elaborate hoax if it was.

If I ever meet Joan, I'll have to thank her for her creativity.

There were more messages, but I'd gotten the gist. I had screwed up, royally.

Frank must have walked back; he was standing by the bushes where I had been watching earlier.

He opened the door to my convertible, pressed the knob to push the passenger seat back, threw himself in and quietly closed the door.

"Tony, they must have known we were watching. I finally walked back when my car was blocked and a truck with no markings rode past me, looked like they had just left the building. Seemed like it was refrigerated, you know, thick walls. Could have been delivering more bodies."

He'd been talking so fast I couldn't get a word in until finally he drew a breath.

"Frankie, how many bodies did Elsa say they had at the West Palm morgue, maybe three or four?"

"Right, there must be more than one morgue supplying corpses," he hesitated like he was trying to come up with an answer, "but how many times can you get a call from the State House to release a body? How many morgues and people can you get involved?"

He pointed through the bushes toward the cement building. "They could have brought in a half dozen or more in the truck that looked like it left the lot. Maybe there was more than one truck. I was gone close to an hour. Where they getting all the bodies? Not all from the morgue."

I wasn't sure how to comfortably bring up the subject of Elsa, and what Kate described as her long time lover. But it seemed important and would distract from my explanation of how long it can take to finish a cone from Sprinkles.

"Did you ask Elsa if there had been other bodies removed too soon, like Jimmy?"

He smiled at the mention of her name, "Yes, I spoke with her a couple of times. She said there were no other quickie ins and outs like Jimmy."

"Did you tell her about this building?"

"I did, and she was a little quiet, then asked if I had been inside. I said you had, but the night watchman came before you could see anything specific.

Then said she had someone in her office; she'd call me back."

She's involved for sure, I thought. "How long ago?"

He checked his watch. "Been several hours now. Said she'd call right back. Funny, she hasn't called."

Not funny, ha ha, I thought, she's up to her ears in this. She may have been the one who told the people inside, or the guys delivering the stiffs, that we were at the morgue asking questions.

I opened my door and stepped out of the car as though I were checking out the street, then leaned back in.

"Seems what was going to happen already has. Let's get a bite to eat and try and sort things out. I'll drop you at your car and meet you at Buccan."

I let Frank off at his car, which was no longer blocked. He drove off first; I waved but didn't follow.

CHAPTER 25

Advice from Perez

Instead of following Frank, I speed dialed my pal Sergeant Sonja Perez.

No answer, so I left a message. "Perez, I've got a problem. Can you check on a couple of things for me on the QT? I need the owner of the cement building at the rear of the parking lot on Peruvian."

I paused to make it seem like another reasonable request, then continued, "Wonder if you know any investigations of organ harvesting in Palm Beach County?"

I felt the odds of this being a lab to take organs for resale were slim. It didn't match Jimmy's case, which seemed to be an insurance scam, and the neurosurgeon wouldn't be cutting out kidneys. But the harvesting question would get her attention.

Sure enough, I'd only driven a couple hundred yards and was close to the corner of South County when the phone buzzed. "Not more dead bodies that Palm Beach's finest don't even know about, I hope." She was chuckling.

"No, Perez, but something very strange is going on. I can't tell you too much 'cause a lot is guess work."

To answer your message Tony, "I'll check on the building, but the answer to the body parts is yes, but not by our department. The feds are all over it. Seems when the Oxycontin scam was closed down; they found this body parts business was a part of it. Some may be still operating. Problem is, some well-known hospitals were unwittingly involved and they're trying to hush it up. What I've told you has been in the papers. My job would be on the line if I told you what I really know."

I took that as a yes to my original question, but what my real question was, was what about Joan and the brain surgeon?

While I was trying to figure out how to bring it up, she said, "Tony, I did check again on Joan's contact at the State House to find out who may have released Jimmy's body. So far I've gotten nowhere. Even Congressman Murphy's office denies any contact. What about you? See her at any more funerals?"

Good old Perez, sometimes I think she can read minds. Of course, mine is easy.

The valet waved me around in front of Buccan and was holding the door to my car. I stepped out and walked back to the corner to continue our conversation.

"Joan Diamond attending funerals? Yes, but it all doesn't make much sense. My guess is the feds who handled the Oxycontin scam are probably involved in this body part investigation, but have you heard anything about experiments where they're operating on brains?"

There was a long pause, and then she said, "What does this have to do with the building on Peruvian? You were talking like it was a body parts shop. What's the deal?"

"I had a lunch with Kate at Jean-Pierre. She gave me a lot of negative stuff about this woman at the morgue: Elsa, the woman Frank seems quite involved with, plus a guy who works with her."

She had given another, "Oh, how nice," when I mentioned Frank and a girlfriend.

"Maybe not," I said. "It's possible she's somehow in on the scam, plus Kate thinks Elsa has a very cozy relationship with this guy who works with her at the morgue."

I hesitated, and then hit her with the big one. "I went to the Grill to find out if Rebecca knew anything about Joan. Turns out

Joan was there and left with a guy who's a neurosurgeon. I followed them to the building on Peruvian. Joan and the brain guy went in together, and about a half hour later came back out, but not alone. The fellow that works at the morgue with Elsa follows them out."

Perez cut in, "The one who Kate says has an involvement with Frank's new girlfriend?"

"You got it. Now I don't know who's on first, let alone third."

"And you don't want Frank, your best pal, who lost a wife not that far back, to get hurt again."

She was silent, then continued, "If you tell him and you're wrong, he resents you for killing a great love story. If you're right and don't say anything, he could be hurt, and not just emotionally.

You haven't told Frank about the morgue guy leaving the building have you?"

"No, only about Joan and the brain guy. I knew if I told Frank, he'd tell Elsa, and if she's involved, our cover is gone."

"Don't say anything yet, Tony. Let me see what I can find out about the Fed's investigation of these body part shops and whether one of my friends at the State House knows about Joan Diamond's neurosurgeon."

CHAPTER 26

Buccan

I headed in figuring Frank would be waiting and cursing.
I got the waiting part right. But cursing and missing me, no way. Frank was standing to the left of the entrance talking with Delaila, as pretty as her name, and Lisa, a natural 10. She's the hostess with the million-dollar smile. The guy doing the hiring definitely knows what he's doing.

The girls noticed me and smiled, then spotted a couple at the door and headed over to greet them.

Thinking of Perez's final comment, I decide to ask the obvious: "Did Elsa call you back?"

The way he looked again at his cell told me no, but instead of a direct answer, I got: "After that first time she met the sisters for drinks, Elsa has had several conversations, but mainly with Rebecca's sister Stacey; in fact, they met this morning over coffee. Elsa said Stacey gave her a little more background on Joan, the morgue and funerals. But when Elsa threw in Jimmy — his being down and out, the hit and run, Joan picking up the body — Stacey gave her a strange look and asked, 'You are talking about James Patterson?' Elsa said, 'Yes why?' to which Stacey replied, 'Oh, nothing, just know the name.' But it was clear she knew more and wasn't telling."

He paused and scratched his chin like he sometimes does when confused, "How could she connect to Jimmy, other than seeing him in his disheveled state getting coffee at Starbucks after sleeping who knows where? But if that was all, why wouldn't she say so?"

"I don't know, Frankie. Between her and Elsa, one with the Agency, one whose husband was killed working there, I'm sure they could both get a little paranoid."

I still hadn't told Frank about the three of them leaving the building the other night, and wasn't sure how to approach it.

"I assume you told Elsa about the building. What did she think? Any insights?"

"She seemed surprised when I said the building was in Palm Beach. Course, like the rest of us, has wondered where they took Jimmy, and if there are others."

He checked his cell again, "After five. Funny she hasn't called back."

"Call her again. She's probably just getting out of work. Maybe she'd like to join us."

He stepped over toward the high top at the front window, I assumed to avoid my hearing all that mushy early relationship stuff that even guys in their mid-eighties disburse.

Taylor had placed a Dewar's and water on the bar, given me a little wave of hello, and was busy setting up for another busy night in Palm Beach's newest hotspot.

I was getting more and more nervous for Frank, and wondering what excuse Elsa, who had rushed Frank off the phone as soon as he told her about the building, would come up with next. That is if she even answers his call.

He was back in a minute. "She's in her car, was heading over to do a little shopping on Worth; she'll be here in ten minutes."

CHAPTER 27

Confessions

I had to admit that Elsa was a hot little number. Two young guys, probably still in their twenties, had come in just behind her and stopped to watch her walk our way. She was sexually appealing — in a nice way.

Frank got the big hug and kiss on the lips, which, I had to say looked very genuine. I got a little less hug and the kiss on the cheek.

I pointed to the high top. "Let's sit here were we can talk. Frank said you're a Pinot Grigio girl. I'll get you a drink."

As I placed the chilled glass and napkin in front of her and sat facing them, I noticed a different look, like the switch she had made at the morgue, from friendly chatter to a business-like explanation of the embalming process.

She started in, "I have a confession to make. But Tony, you must swear what I tell you to secrecy."

Just me, I thought. Do you have Frank wrapped so tight around your little finger you don't have to worry about him?

But I kept still.

She started in, "I have been concerned for some time about strange things going on at the morgue, like Joan Diamond picking up the body early. When you two showed up, I thought, 'Finally, I can involve someone else and hopefully get some answers.'

I'm never sure if it's my paranoia because of my husband's strange death, or something real, but I needed to involve someone else to find out, and you two showed up at the right time. Of course, having an attraction to Frank made you two an easy choice."

She sipped her wine, gave his hand a little squeeze, and broke away from the serious lecture pose. "I just didn't realize how much, and the wonderful journey I would embark on."

The lecture look resumed. "I have known for some time that Adam, my longtime friend at the morgue, is into some strange cult things. As far as I knew, it was nothing really illegal. But when Frank told me about the building in Palm Beach, I suspected Adam might be involved. And if he was, maybe I could prevent him from getting into serious trouble."

She shook her head. "Might be too late. I learned early on about computer hacking from my husband, and am, in fact, quite good at it. I easily got into his computer and found several radical YouTube speeches from some Al Qaeda website."

She threw up her hands and shrugged. "Then on Shiite websites he's reading about creating a Manchurian candidate type plot. All these people in a catatonic or hypnotized state stationed in major cities all over the country. On a certain day they'll be set free to wreak havoc on the population, poisoning water supplies with bacteria, E. coli — anything that spreads and causes a painful death — all kinds of wild stuff."

She paused. "It seems unreal, but I saw this craziness on his computer with my own eyes. Adam is definitely involved. The only saving grace is Adam is so scattered, he needs a note to go to the store. He could never plan or carry out anything one tenth of this scale, but he's easily influenced and could get in over his head without knowing the consequences."

It seemed I had been wrong about her, and now I wished I'd told Frank more. They were sitting very close. Frank was to my left, making it difficult to not look his way, but I did manage to focus on her face and the wall behind her, trying not to look at Frank, who I knew would be annoyed.

I started in, what I didn't tell you before, because I knew you and Adam were friends, was I saw him come out of the building with Joan after I followed them the other night."

Without looking directly, it appeared he was shaking his head and scowling.

I felt it best to keep talking. "I have spoken on several occasions with our friend Sergeant Perez of the Palm Beach Police, who tells me Joan Diamond has multiple contacts at the State House and isn't sure who she called to release the body.

Perez isn't certain Joan is involved, but to me, clearly she is. I saw her leaving with Adam, who, based on what you're telling me, is at least a wannabe terrorist.

Who do we call? Who do we contact?"

Elsa reached across and patted my hand. "That's easy. I'll connect you with Stacey. She's much closer and more up to date on what's going on than I ever was." She stopped for a moment, and then continued with anger taking over her voice, which was getting louder and starting to break when she finished with, "Thanks to the CIA's 'protect the little woman' philosophy, my husband is dead and I will never be told why."

Frank put his arm around her and pulled her close. A true gesture of love I thought, considering she was talking about a man, dead for years, who she still clearly loved.

Feeling a bit out of touch with what was going on with these two, I needed an escape route. I waved to a woman I didn't know on the dining room side of the bar, stood up and pointed in her direction, not looking back to see if the two lovers were even paying attention.

They weren't.

CHAPTER 28

Excuse for an Old Connection

By the time I got to the door, I had my cell phone out and had speed dialed Perez. This new wrinkle about websites and brainwashing labs all over the country, if true, was serious. We had to let someone know, and Perez would deal with it properly. All the years I had known her, she never went off half-cocked, always weighed all the possibilities, one of which, I hated to consider, was that Elsa was either being miss-lead, or prone to exaggerate.

My other issue was seeing my best pal Frank, so content in a seemingly sound relationship, versus, as Kate inferred, my whimsical relationship with bimbos. Plus, my immediately proving her point, by going to the Grill and ending up in bed with my ice cream date. Eva was certainly no bimbo, but clearly making Kate's point about me.

Compared to me, Eva's thoughtful, mature decision-making about her future life only accentuated the craziness of my day-to-day, or maybe hour-to-hour thought process.

Time to fish or cut bait as the less crude expression goes.

It had been over two years since I had seen Gabriella.

I needed to talk to someone who had the authority to check into our problem with the zombie caper and give me some womanly advice. Perez knew well the tale of my bittersweet romance and my rescue by Emily.

"Tony, I'm getting nowhere — nada on this State House body release bit."

I was silent for a moment then gave her an abbreviated version of Elsa hacking into Adam's computer, which she kind of shrugged off with a laugh and a "seems a little far-fetched to me. I'll try and find who in the government handles Al Qaeda zombies."

Then I delivered my, "Well Sergeant, I've been thinking, the one person I know in undercover government work, not well, but well enough, is the woman with the FBI that pulled me away in the Paris airport."

"Emily Jones," she shot back. "Plus, maybe she can reconnect you with Gabriella; you've never been the same since she left."

I hadn't ever really thought about it in those terms, but it was true. Probably my first really committed relationship since my just out of college marriage to Elizabeth, where love finally trumped lust.

I was quietly thinking, Sonja Perez had always set me straight; Emily was definitely the place to start.

"Tony, the answer is yes."

"I haven't asked the question yet."

"Don't need to; there's an outside chance Emily can help you find the right person in Washington to talk to, and wasn't her Paris unit keeping an eye on Gabriella's father and that whole Italian Mafioso connection? Didn't she say they were laying off him because he was trying to turn it legit? Do you know how to connect with her?"

"Not sure, but I could start with the Paris office. Maybe reach the fellow that looked after me when I was chasing after Gabriella: Pierre."

"Try him Tony, and I'll check my sources. I have a good pal with the FBI in Tampa. He'll know where to locate her if Pierre doesn't, or can't say."

Paris is six hours ahead, making it close to midnight. Better wait 'till morning. I headed back in to find the lovebirds where I left them. They had ordered a bottle of pinot grigio and the mushroom pizza.

Frank was uncharacteristically nibbling on a slice and offered me a piece. Not that he's stingy with food or drinks, but to see a guy who could easily down three full pizzas merely nibbling? Wow, love does strange things to men.

Elsa asked, "Did you speak with Sonya about the zombies, about the Al Qaeda connection?"

I didn't want to say she sloughed it off, so I said, "Yes, thought it very interesting, was going to check and see if she could reach a friend to see who should be advised."

The place was filling up with a generally younger crowd and a few faces I remember as regulars at the Grill during the old days. There were few women I knew to chat with, but I was itchy. Gabriella, the zombie deal, the possible Al Qaeda connection; drinking and small talk didn't hack it.

I asked Elsa, "Can you give me a few more details on Adam's Al Qaeda or Shiite connection? Was he just researching, studying them, or did it look like real connections?"

"Tony, seems if you saw him at the lab with the Diamond woman and a brain surgeon that's a pretty good indication. But I told you before, Stacey at Main Street News is still very tuned in to what goes on. She's the best place to start."

She took out her cell. "I'm calling her and will put you on. You need to hook up with her to," she winked, "connect the dots."

When it seemed she had reached her, Elsa leaned back behind Frank and was whispering with her hand over her mouth. Too many years as the wife of an undercover guy made her suspect people were watching; perhaps they were.

She handed me the phone. "It's Stacey. She knows all about you."

I wasn't quite sure what that meant, but took the phone. "Hello, Stacey. Are you free to meet and talk some time?"

I was a little taken back by her reply. "Sure, meet me at Bice in a half hour. I'll be in the Worth Avenue side of the courtyard by the window of the Eye of the Needle shop, wearing red."

I started to reply, but she had hung up.

Meet me in a half hour; I'll be dressed in red? Seemed maybe Elsa and this Stacey had this all arranged in advance.

CHAPTER 29

Stacey

This was getting to be real spy novel stuff. Eye of the Needle is a hip Palm Beach shop with a diverse collection of designer clothes in the Via (In Palm Beach there are no alleys, just Vias) behind Bice that runs through from Worth Avenue to Peruvian. It's about a half block from the lab, by the way, and also the title of a Ken Follette novel and Donald Sutherland spy film.

This is going to be an interesting meeting. Stacey seems to know all about the lab from Elsa, plus I liked the film connection.

Peruvian is one way going in the wrong direction. I decided to park on Worth and come in from the other side to try and observe her before she saw me.

I guessed she'd be coming from West Palm, so I'd be early.

I sat in my car for a minute trying to reconstruct what she already knew from Elsa.

They got close because of the CIA connection. Possibly, she knew everything, including the information Elsa took from Adam's computer. It was kinda dumb of me running to Perez about Emily when Elsa's CIA contacts were already in place, maybe already involved in trying to sort it all out.

Was Emily may be my subconscious hope to connect with Gabriella?

A beat up Oldsmobile pulled up a couple cars in front of me and backed in between a dark blue Bentley convertible and an Aston Martin.

Hey, this is Worth (as in high net worth) Avenue.

A very attractive blond, younger looking than the early forties I expected, got out dressed in a tight fitting, but not flirty, red dress and very high heels to match. Definitely not her spy outfit.

I sat and watched as she checked out the fashions in the windows and casually strolled down the alley.

Once out of sight, I got out and followed. Then, just before she reached the Eye of the Needle, she turned and waved.

"Hello, Tony, so nice to finally meet you."

I was a little taken back. She was clearly watching me watch her.

She hooked her arm in mine. "I'm not much of a drinker, so let's skip Bice and take a look at this building that's causing all the commotion."

She was average height, easily short of my six feet, even in her three-inch heels.

We headed through the alleyway, crossed the street, and walked up the block and into the parking lot next to the lab.

"I prefer the direct approach, don't you Tony?"

Not sure what was next, I nodded, "Oh, sure."

She let go of my arm, climbed the four steps to the loading platform, and pressed the bell.

After a short delay, an elderly fellow in a white coat opened the sliding door a crack. "May I help you?"

"Yes," she said, and handed him a card. "I'm a real estate broker and understand the parking lot and building are for sale. May we come in?"

The gentleman in the coat, clearly a little flustered, said, "I know nothing about those things. We are a government-sponsored testing lab and I am not allowed to let anyone in." He smiled, "I'm sure you understand."

"What division of government?" she asked in what seemed a very soft tone for such a ballsy woman. "I was once with the government myself. I do understand the red tape and secrecy." Stacey put out her hand. "Scarlett Johansson."

"Oh yes, like the movie star," he replied, taking her hand. "We are not able to divulge what we do. Nothing mysterious I assure. That's just the way the government do."

I was thinking. She did look a bit like a Scarlett Johansson and I was wondering what her next move would be, when she said, "Thank you for your time sir. Enjoy the rest of your day," and stepped back from the door.

"Let's go. We have taken this nice man away from his busy day."

We were barely at the street when she said, "Did you notice the slight accent? When and how he said that's the way the government do?"

I had to admit I hadn't.

"And the boots. They're Russian made, but often worn in the Middle East. Plus the accent or pronunciation, all their words tend to end in a vowel. His 'That's the way the government do.' My guess is Damascus. That boot was all the rage there a few years back; it's a Russian design, but made locally. One of the early attempts at free enterprise that actually worked."

She pointed to Bice. "We have a lot to talk about; maybe I will have that drink."

I was impressed and suddenly wondering what I might add to this talk.

We found two seats at the street end of the busy bar and got comfortable. Easy to notice in her heels and bright red dress, the bartender came right over.

"Do you have a Pimms Absinthe?" she asked.

"Interesting, don't get a lot of requests for that one. Let me see." He rattled off the ingredients: "Pimms Absinthe — orange, cucumber, and yeah, I can mix up a little cinnamon sugar." He was smiling to himself for remembering, and at "Scarlett" for adding a little interest to a job that has too many boring beer or Dewar's and water guys like me.

She started in, and in a low whisper said, "I suspect I know what is going on in there. Are you familiar with Scopolamine?"

I shook my head, but it seemed maybe she and Elsa had discussed the lab in depth.

"Scopolamine is the primary active ingredient in Burundanga extracts used by criminals, and has also been used by government intelligence agencies in various countries for interrogation and brainwashing. Scopolamine in that context has been called "truth serum." When a person is under the spell, you just make a verbal suggestion and they follow. Very cool stuff."

She smiled, thanked the bartender for her Pimms, and continued. "The flowers from the Burundanga plant are used as a hallucinogen in Colombia and other South American countries. They mix it in tea, then kind of trip off. The baby seeds from the tree are most dangerous. One nut the size of an acorn has enough to kill fifty people. They soak the seeds in acetone to break it down, strain out the heavy pieces, and then put the mix in a rotary evaporator. It's a similar process to cocaine, but this stuff in powder form is a hundred times stronger."

She stopped, sipped her Pimms, and turned to me. "This part seems a little unreal, but it's a major problem in Columbia. Criminals take a small amount of powder in a very weak form and blow it in the face of a potential victim. The person is immediately put in a hypnotized state and subject to the will of their keeper."

She turned again, put her hand palm up and pretended to blow gently in my face. "If I had a tiny amount of this powder in my palm, you would be completely under my control. This is what these criminals do; they blow a small amount in your face and say, 'Take me to your bank cash machine' or they go to the clerk at the counter. 'Now draw out all your money and give it to me,' or maybe with an attractive woman, 'come to my place and make love to my client.'

Done deal. The person is completely open to suggestion and has no power to resist. Five or six hours later they come to and have zero memory of what occurred. They go to the bank, the money is gone. They ask the teller, and she says, 'Yes, you were here earlier and took out all your money. Here is the slip you signed.'"

"Unbelievable," I said. "So they really are in a zombie state? I must admit I was skeptical about this zombie business, but I do remember reading an article in the Miami Herald about a year ago about a guy who was on an off ramp of the Miami expressway. He was naked and growling while chewing on the face of a homeless man. True story, the police shot the guy. There were photos of the poor guy he attacked, with his face half chewed off."

Stacey was nodding, "Yes, I saw the article. That's probably PCP — angel dust, used as a horse tranquilizer. Makes the user hallucinate, become extremely violent, almost return to a primal state, like an animal. Bad stuff, but not what I suspect they are doing here."

As she was explaining, I remembered Elsa putting down the whole idea of zombie's. Wouldn't she, like Stacey, be familiar with this stuff?

Maybe I was over thinking the whole deal, but obviously these two had talked a lot and were way ahead of me in trying to figure it out.

I nodded. "You read about the drugs that are available in the Amazon rain forest, used by the natives for generations to cure all kinds of ailments. All the money we spend on research, and in some ways these people are years ahead in curing many diseases."

She smiled. "True, and some plants, like beautiful women, are femme fatales. They can be seductively deceiving, like Salome dancing to seduce, or the black widow spider. The Burandanga plant has incredibly beautiful white flowers hanging below its green leaves. It's compared to an angel's skirt, but it is as deadly as it is beautiful. It could send you to heaven real early."

Fascinated by her knowledge of this area, I wondered if she was a member of the drug generation and asked. "Were drugs pretty prolific when you were a teen?"

She shook her head. "No, I grew up in West Texas on a ranch of about twenty acres, with horses. One day when I was about ten or twelve I was out in the corral with my dad, and one of the horses was acting kinda strange. He'd come up real close, his face close to yours, like he was checking you out, and then he'd jump back, rear up on his hind legs and race around like crazy. It was weird, but my dad knew and had us scour the area for plants or flowers the horse may have been eating. We kids brought in dozens of plants and he tested them. Finally, he discovered the horse had eaten one of the drugs in this family of hallucinogens, so we tore up all those plants and burned them."

She sipped her drink and smiled. "I was a curious kid and a good student. I began studying plants, drugs, and this whole area. Eventually I got the attention of a professor at the University. He encouraged me, and worked with me on this study."

She faced me and smiled. "Well, it turned out he taught languages. I got interested in Chinese, maybe because it wasn't taught in the public schools and I wanted to be different. I was an avid reader, lot of biographies. My favorite woman in history was the Russian psychologist Lou Andreas-Salome. She was the toast of Vienna back in the 1920s, believed that women are the naturally superior sex. Incredibly smart, she studied under Freud and was close to Frederick Nietzsche, Paul Ree and the Russian poet Rilke. I wanted to be like her."

She smiled to herself and sighed as though having a nice memory.

"What were you thinking?" I asked.

"What do you mean?"

"Just then, you left me for a moment and were back there."

"Oh, yes." She tipped her head back and smiled. My professor friend was much older, died last year. He was my first love and lover."

I said, "I know of Andreas-Salome," and smiled, but went no further.

I didn't want to get into how closely she may have modeled herself after this woman who didn't just believe in women's superiority, she was a serious polygamous with tremendous power over men. She had an affair with Freud, lived in earlier times in a ménage a trois with philosophers Frederick Neitzsche and nihilist Paul Ree, and had hundreds of lovers.

I listened as she continued her story. "Then an opportunity in China opened up. My professor friend got a call from IBM. They needed translators; he recommended me, so off I went at age 18 to

China. The CIA naturally interviewed us when we got home. The rest is history."

"Fascinating story. That's how you met Leslie Weiss, who worked for Frank?"

She smiled and nodded. "Nice woman. We met on my first trip. She had been to China many times before. We keep in touch still."

"But Stacey, if this stuff only lasts for a few hours, how are they keeping guys like Jimmy in there for days?"

"Hold on, Tony. We don't even know really what specific drugs they are using. May not even be Scopolamine. They could even be taking these people and using them as guinea pigs to test some new combinations."

She sat back on her bar stool and smiled." Maybe we could use our own femme fatale, our own enchantress, to get to someone inside."

"Who do we get?"

"She smiled, and said, "Leave that up to me."

"Who does she enchant?"

She smiled as though she was going to enjoy this next step.

"Adam at the morgue."

I thought about her idol, Lou Andreas-Salome.

Hey, maybe she can pull it off.

Or was it already in process? Clearly, Stacey and Elsa had worked this whole scheme out before I took her to the lab door, before we stopped at Bice for her Pimms Absinthe, and before she explained her theory on how this whole zombie drug thing works. Good chance they were already working her femme fatale on an unsuspecting Adam.

I wondered how this had evolved. Had Elsa somehow felt that because of my work as a detective I was the lead guy in this mystery? That she would feel more comfortable continuing with their plan if I had at least met Stacey and been made aware of what they were doing?

Having met her, I realized their definition of "aware" probably differed from mine. It appeared I would be as aware as they chose to let me be, which, for the Adam piece, would turn out to be very little.

After Stacey's mentioning Adam as their prey, I re-thought Elsa's outlining of his job history. He clearly had, as she had explained, a fascination with death. His first career had been with her family's funeral business. From there he came straight to the morgue. Plus, his oft stated comment that "Life is a brief stop in the endless abyss of eternity."

Elsa had portrayed Adam as strange, but until I saw him and could observe him more closely, I figured she meant he was just a little different, kind of normal weird. Someone we excuse with a, "Hey, it takes all kinds" comment. But whether he was involved because of a strong political belief or just a fun way to find out about death, he was definitely weirder and much more involved than I first thought. Clearly, if anyone would be attracted to zombies, he would.

As for Elsa, Frank, in one of his many unsolicited lectures on women, had often said legs, tits, and a great smile are all important. But ultimately the most important attribute to look for in a woman is her disposition, her temperamental makeup. Does she sweat the small stuff? It seemed that Elsa, other than a few tears and some temporary anger when talking about her dead husband — not exactly small stuff — seemed to have this calm temperament that Frank had lectured me on.

I thought about his third wife, Helene. She had been the perfect match, but had died of cancer several years before. I had been hoping he'd finally find the right one. Perhaps he had.

Then there was Stacey, perfectly dressed for her slim but shapely figure, and in spite of the cool dark rimmed glasses, not trying to be Palm Beach glamorous. She had a great smile and interesting blue eyes, but there was something else. As soon as she spoke, you forget the looks (not easy for me) and realized her most attractive attribute was similar to her favorite woman in history — her intellect.

She was just plain interesting. Any further comparisons to Lou Andreas-Salomé and how she used this power over men — I wasn't prepared to speculate on.

CHAPTER 30

Sorting Life Out

I hadn't slept well. Thoughts of my ice cream date with Eva had focused less on our time in bed and more on her mature approach to life statement. "Sex is momentary and as the yearnings fade with age, the desire for sex dims." I thought again about Kate's bimbo lecture, "if Gabriella is the one, go after her."

Even Gabriella, who loved me, left because of the duty she felt for her family.

I got dressed, slinked into Green's, avoiding eye contact with anyone who might inquire about my wanton existence, grabbed my coffee, and walked the short distance to the beach.

We'd caught the tail end of the winter storms whose waves and heavy surf had dragged the sand back from the wall, lowering and flattening the beach. Now, at high tide, the ocean came all the way to the wall, and even at dead low there wasn't much beach left. The change was causing cross currents that flowed sideways to the beach. This, added to the strong waves, made it difficult for all but the strongest swimmers. Getting onto the beach had become a difficult slide down a steep cliff of sand. Climbing or crawling back up is even worse.

It seemed even the power of the ocean was helping to accentuate the insignificance of my existence.

I sat on the wall, sipped my coffee, and stared out at the deserted beach and thought again about Gabriella.

I checked my cell. Seven a.m. in Palm Beach, one p.m. in Paris.

Pierre's number was still there from the prior day. I tried the speed dial.

"Bonjour, Pierre, parler."

"Pierre, it's me, Tony Tauck. I need to reach Emily Jones. Is she available?"

Pierre hesitated, not wanting to reveal her whereabouts without her permission. "Oui, Mr. Tauck, she is not available. May I reach her and have her call you?"

"Yes, Pierre, there's something important we need to talk about that has to do with security in this country."

"Securite, Oh mon. I will have her call you right back. Good-bye."

CHAPTER 31

Elsa Intrigues Adam

After the fact, I learned what these two had been up to. It seems Elsa had caught up with Adam while having coffee and found him engrossed in an article in the Sidney Herald about a woman who had been accused of killing a six-year-old boy by use of sorcery.

Adam had excitedly read her excerpts of the story, where the accused woman had been murdered and cannibalized for her act of sorcery. He eagerly explained there is a law against sorcery in Australia and it is often used as a defense when a person is accused of murder: "I killed a sorcerer."

This discussion of a belief most of us thought to be resolved 350 plus years ago in Salem, Massachusetts, led to a dialogue of the afterlife of witches and cannibals, allowing Elsa to casually bring up her friend Joyce, known to us as Stacey, who she described as having a near death experience.

Adam was fascinated by the tale and had to know more. Almost hourly he had made a point of dropping by her office or catching her in the hallways to discover more about her friend, each time pressing her for more information. And each time Elsa dropped some other tidbit, such as traveling at the speed of light through a long tunnel with bright colors at the end, or her soul floating above her body, or looking down at herself in her death bed.

A few more tales and Adam was pressing Elsa to meet her friend.

Finally, she relented and told him that Joyce's favorite hangout was the Tiki Bar at the Key Lime restaurant in Lantana. She cautioned him. "Don't bring it up. Let me introduce the subject."

CHAPTER 32

Old Key Lime House

The Old Key Lime House is an easy 15-minute ride south on Dixie. Its relaxed series of bars, thatched roofs, open dining areas, and tables for two seem to go on forever is definitely designed for a good time.

No glimpse of the water here. Old Key Lime is like sitting on the dock enjoying a meal that is easily as good as what we get in Palm Beach, but without the Palm Beach prices.

Stacey said hello to Wayne, the owner, who sat with his pal, AC Brooks, talking tackle and bait. Both are serious sports fishermen and adventurous world travelers. AC is a writer of adventure tales about Shagball, who has an early morning TV show on fishing, and his midget sidekick, Tangles. Wayne, just back from Afghanistan, was passing around photos.

After a brief discussion, Wayne pointed toward the bar on the dock. "Tall, skinny, kinda weird looking guy with an attractive older woman, I think looking for you. They're at the bar on the dock, down at the east end."

Elsa saw Stacey and waved her over. "Joyce, this is my good friend Adam. We work together at the morgue."

She stood, gave Stacey a hug, and pointed. "Let's take that table out on the dock."

Tripping over his feet as he got up, Adam extended a hand.

"Hello, nice to meet you."

Elsa sat down pulling Stacey next to her so the two women were on one side, with Adam directly across from Stacey in her very revealing mesh tank top.

Stacey sat quietly staring intently into Adam's, eyes while trying not to smile at Elsa's made-up story of their meeting years ago at a séance. She explained how Stacey had been hypnotized into a deep trance, sending her back to her childhood accident where she thought she was dead; Stacey, all the while sitting in a dreamlike state, appearing to recall and feel the made-up tale. Only occasionally would she interject a comment or emphasize a point. The stories went on for some time, with Adam listening and nodding, while also quite engrossed in Stacey's chest, where a gold pendant swung slowly back and forth as she motioned with her hands to emphasize points of her story.

Finally she reached out and took his hands in hers. Holding his wrists and applying pressure, she was able to relax him into a hypnotic state.

As later described by Elsa, Stacey's pendant and pressure on his wrists put Adam into a dream state, increasing his attraction and her control over him. She had studied Salome, and in some ways had become her.

Soon Adam was telling them his deepest thoughts and desires, the strongest of which had become his attraction to Stacey and his wish to introduce her to his world.

Feeling she had him under her influence, and under the pretense of checking her watch, she counted backward from ten to one while holding his hand to her lips. At zero she had stood, kissed him gently on the cheek and walked quickly to the exit.

CHAPTER 33

The Boston Marathon

Elsa and Frank were glued to the television at her Slade apartment watching coverage of the manhunt for the Boston Marathon bombers.

Elsa saw Stacey's name flash on her phone, stood, and walked away from the couch and TV.

She spoke quietly into her cell with Stacey, who, after asking if Frank was listening, was reassured by Elsa he wasn't.

"Frank has been married three times," Elsa explained, "his hearing is a product of evolution."

"Evolution?" asked Stacey. "In what way?"

Elsa laughed, "Think about it. A man, newly married, saying 'yes dear' to pacify his wife, while all he is really interested in is focusing on whatever sport he's watching on TV.

With each new wife, he's better at it. By the third, his listening level is down to a quarter. With me it's nearly nonexistent."

Stacey laughed, and then continued, "I met Adam at Bice. We had a long talk. I explained my family ranch and knowledge of drugs. He was anxious to impress me and talked about his theories of life after death. Finally, after a few drinks and some minor petting, we went for a walk to, guess where?"

"Really!" was Elsa's reply as she stepped into the kitchen to get away from Frank and the TV chatters.

"Yes, I thought I might have to use something more powerful, but he's smitten and wanted to impress. I was a little concerned it might be the same guard who came to the door when I was with Tony, but it was someone different. He recognized Adam and let us in."

"And?" asked Elsa, anxiously awaiting some breakthrough.

"The fellow left us and headed into the back section, which was closed off and locked. We were in a big room, dimly lit. It seemed to be a large laboratory with computerized equipment, shelves of chemical compounds and several large metal tables.

Adam explained it was set up similar to the morgue, with the front section used for experiments. The back area, which was closed off, was where they kept the bodies for doing what he described as medical research.

I asked about the zombie state and how they keep them at that level. He said they have a patch on the arm that releases the Scopolamine powder every eight hours to keep them in that hypnotic/zombie state."

She stopped for a moment as though thinking about how to express her next thought.

"He avoided taking me into the back area; made excuses that made no sense, even for him. When I asked specific questions about the bodies' appearance, he stumbled over the answers. I expect it may be off limits; he may never have been allowed back there."

"You know Adam better than I. Do you think this place is just another morgue to him, with medical experiments? Cause that's how he talks. I mean, he does have this fascination with these Al Qeada type groups, though I'm not sure the group he follows most closely is even Al Qeada — seems more Shiite than Sunni, but is it a game to him? Are they just using him? He'll be the fall guy at the end?"

She paused. "Is he interested in blowing people up to get his 72 virgins?"

"No, no" Elsa laughed, "I don't see him praying five times a day and reading the Qu'ran. He's fascinated with death and the afterlife; thinks this is a way to find out."

"Well," continued Stacey, "The more I see of this operation, the more I think someone has a lot more in mind than experiments. Think about it: here we are watching the news about two men influenced over time by radical Islamists to blow people up."

"Crazy stuff," added Elsa. "You think this is connected?"

Before Stacey could reply, Elsa continued, "I see your point. Rather than going through that long process of creating these seemingly lone wolf incidents, they create an army of these zombie's, maybe to be let loose in different cities on a particular day, vests filled with explosives, anthrax, or whatever."

"Exactly," said Stacey. "A dozen here in Palm Beach. A dozen or more in a bunch of other cities across the country. All let loose on May Day, Memorial Day, the 4th of July or whenever. Lot easier to control when you don't have the FBI checking their trips out of the country to see what training camps they attend, plus what radical websites and YouTube videos they're watching. There is nothing to check, no leads to follow."

"Yes," said Elsa. "Plus, if they survive, they don't remember anything."

Then she added, "I suspect they are using Adam and people like him to get the bodies, and when they get ready to act, or maybe before, he'll be history."

Stacey was about to hang up when Elsa asked, "Where are they getting the bodies? They can't all be coming from this morgue or others. It's too complicated."

"I asked Adam about that, and he said something about closed OxyContin clinics, but didn't get into detail. That certainly could be a source. Scumbags that oversold OxyContin can't have a lot of concern for life. Could be supplying severe addicts to this program.

I tried to get Adam to tell me more, but the guy is so ADHD I got nowhere."

Elsa chuckled. "Adam could be a poster boy for attention deficit and hyperactivity. I can't see him sitting still long enough to study the Qu'ran, let alone remembering to pray five times a day. We have to find a way to extract him from this deal before his ADHD is cured permanently."

Stacey jumped in, "Joan is kind of a mystery woman in this whole mix. If this is more than just a lab for this brain guy to do his experiments; I don't picture Joan blowing up buildings either."

She paused, and then continued, "My manager at the store, Briana, is "old money" Palm Beach. I've seen her chatting with Joan in the store; I'll see if she knows anything."

CHAPTER 34

Back in Davos, a Random Connection

Emily was a little surprised, but delighted by the call. Pierre had been one of her favorites when she ran the Paris office. He had little formal education, but very street smart, which, in their business, is often more important.

Pierre was merely following protocol by contacting Emily for permission before telling Tony where she was or how to make contact.

Though he had asked for her, Emily guessed his conversation might eventually get around to Gabriella.

Tony had no way of knowing the two women were already in close contact.

"Thank you for calling me with Mr. Tauck's number, Pierre. Do give my fond wishes to your wife, and hug the twin girls for me. I bet they are growing like weeds."

She hung up the phone, leaned back in the lounge chair and smiled. In a romantic relationship herself, she was now handed a chance to reunite the former lovers. What could be more fitting and fun?

She gazed out from the balcony at the mountains, now empty of all but a few die-hard skiers, and thought about her secret friend, Gabriella.

"Was Tony really trying to make contact with Emily, or using her as an excuse to reconnect with Gabriella?

It didn't matter. She would find a way to get them together.

CHAPTER 35

Main Street News

"She is a very complex woman; always marched to a different drummer," added Briana in response to Stacey's inquiry about Joan Diamond. "I know her, not as a best friend, but forever. We played on the Palm Beach Day School field hockey team."

Briana, who manages the Main Street News, where the town's full- and part-time residents go for newspapers, magazines, and a great selection of books, nodded to herself as though remembering. "She was a grade ahead of me. Tough competitor, hated to lose, but fair."

She pointed to her office in the back of the store. "Let's go where we can talk."

They walked back through the racks, holding what has to be the largest selection of magazines in the state. Past the foreign section, Paris Match, Point De Vue, Der Spiegel and then, interestingly, side by side were copies of Philosophy Now and Messages from God.

Briana sat and pointed to the second chair as Stacey closed the door.

"I remember she had this Haitian nanny that picked her up and dropped her at school. I'm curious. What is your interest; something to do with your old job?"

Stacey nodded and shrugged her shoulders as if to say maybe, maybe not.

"Is Tony Tauck involved?"

Stacey was a little taken back by the question, "Why would you ask that?"

"Just my woman's intuition."

Seeing the puzzled look on Stacey's face, she laughed. "I know him well; we are both of Italian background.

He says, other than his mother, I make the world's best lasagna. He loves my sauces, probably has some in his fridge as we speak. Plus, he came in a few days ago and was asking me the same questions about Joan."

"What else did he tell you?"

"He asked a lot about the nanny from Haiti who used to take Joan to funerals."

"You knew about that?"

"Sure, it was a joke with all the kids. But she's been a big supporter of Haitian people, particularly after the earthquake a few years ago.

Had a couple big fundraisers — one at The Breakers, one at Mar-A-Lago."

What else did Tony ask you?"

"Asked about her politics. Asked if I remember any changes when her Haitian nanny died."

She thought a moment. "Seemed he was hinting that Joan might have become more radical after the nanny died. I thought about it after he left. I'd say definitely, yes."

"Really; why?"

"Joan somehow blamed herself for the woman's death. She had a steady boyfriend at the time, was involved with this guy, and wasn't paying attention. You know the age.

It was a typical government bureaucratic error. The poor woman had been in the country for 10 years. Was perfectly legal, but somehow her immigration status was questioned.

She didn't want to bother Joan, whose family connections could have made a call and fixed it in a minute. Plus, she was scared.

The woman had grown up under the dictator, Papa Doc, who routinely tortured and executed anyone who disagreed with him.

She was afraid, didn't trust the police, and fled to avoid the issue; was killed in a car crash.

Joan was devastated. For all intents and purposes, the nanny was her mother and best friend."

Briana hesitated, "She and I weren't very best pals, but it's a small town. I saw her in school, at sports, at parties, plus we have the Shiny Sheet that tells all. If she came to the store today, she'd stop to chat, ask about my family, that sort of thing."

She paused a moment. "But it always seemed like there were two Joans. After the nanny died she was kind of out of sight for a while. Maybe did get a little radicalized. Seemed one day she was campaigning for causes, raising money for the poor in Haiti one day, and the next day hanging out with friends who were pretty extreme."

"Like how?"

"Like a couple in the group who called themselves the Freedom from Oppression Party (FOP) were later convicted of trying to blow up the federal building in Tallahassee. They had left a truck bomb similar to the Oklahoma City bombing, with one thousand pounds of ammonium nitrate fertilizer and some type of methane racing fuel in the garage under the building. Fortunately it was discovered before it went off.

Some thought she was kept out of it by family money and connections. No one but Joan knows how closely she was involved, but she sure was friendly with the guys that went to jail."

She stopped as though she was trying to connect the pieces. "But then she worked as a volunteer after 9/11, out three nights a week in uniform down in Delray. That's not someone who hates her country. Possible these radical types took advantage of her in a down period after the death of her friend."

Stacey was listening and nodding. "People change."

The phone rang. "Got to get this." Briana picked up the phone and held her hand over the speaker.

"She sure isn't pleased with the guy in the White House. Might do about anything to uncover something that would bring him down."

Stacey nodded, then stood up and left.

CHAPTER 36

Emily, the Matchmaker

After the call from Pierre, Emily had contacted Joseph, avoiding any direct calls to Gabriella. Much as she was well liked and respected in her job, there were always those looking to get ahead by putting someone else down.

Gabriella had been traveling, but arrived to the message and called her friend.

"Remember the dream you had about a week ago, the first night you arrived?'

Gabriella blushed at the memory, "Yes, of course. Why?"

"It may have been foreshadowing. Anthony has been trying to contact me. Said it was business, but I expect the conversation will probably drift around to you. I knew you were planning to return, and I wanted to speak with you before I called him back."

Trying unsuccessfully to withhold her excitement, Gabriella said, "When will you call?"

"I have a private line," she chuckled. "I use it only for top secret government business. I'll call him as soon as you can get over here."

A few minutes later they were sitting in Emily's private office with the phone on speaker while Emily dialed the number.

"Hello, Tony. This is Emily Jones returning your call. How may I help you?"

I had been sitting at home going through a file my friend Jim had left at my place several years back, and had come upon an old copy of Philosophy Now.

I was struggling through an article comparing Oscar Wilde and Friederich Nietzsche, which Jim had marked up with all sorts of notes in the margin. They say the left brain is logical, the right side is creative. I was wondering what brain/personality combination could possibly try and understand Oscar and Freddie with one side of his brain, and on the other have virtually no sense when it came to women or money.

I put down the file and took a deep breath.

"Emily, so nice to hear your voice again. Been over two years since that lovely meeting in the Paris Airport."

"Yes, Tony." She winked at Gabriella. "You were pursuing that woman." She emphasized "that woman" as though she was something to steer clear of.

"Yes, Gabriella." I was planning to continue by saying "the love of my life," but sensed something in Emily's tone and changed the subject. "I called to ask your advice about a very sensitive matter."

I went on to explain the bodies in what seemed to be a zombie state, and after seeing the Marathon bombing, feared these people could be used in a very negative way. I ended with, "We were unable to determine who to contact."

"I am not as familiar with the drugs they use, but am aware of the problem. I have a friend in Columbia. I know of the dust blown in their faces and having to obey. I can make a few private calls and see if anyone is aware of such a plot, and whom you might best contact. I do have a friend in the Tampa office."

Gabriella, sensing the conversation might be coming to a close, nudged her friend. Emily held a finger to her lips. "Tony, this could be something only slightly illegal and a local issue, or it could be a huge national plot. We need to be careful to involve the right people. I will call right away and get back to you."

I started to say, "Look forward to hearing from you," and was ready to hang up when she said, "I know you were quite taken by Gabriella. I supposed you have moved on with your life?"

Eager to express myself to someone so intimately involved on the day of our final meeting, I blurted out, "A day never goes by when I don't think of her. She is a most incredible woman. I know I can't be with her due to her family issues, but I was spoiled. No one else half measures up."

Emily half passed the phone to Gabriella, who waved it off.

"Well Tony, while I'm working on your potential zombie problem, I might be able to make contact with Gabriella. If she's interested should I try to reconnect you?"

The 'if she's interested" caused a slight anxiety, but I answered, "Of course."

"I'll see if I can make contact," she replied.

She hung up the phone, swung her chair around to face Gabriella, and gave her a smiling thumbs up, "After 9/11, our director has worked hard to eliminate the 'protect your own turf' attitude between offices, but some still exists. My advantage is I'm over here in Davos and not competing for big scores. Maybe I'll catch a break for Tony."

CHAPTER 37

Connecting the Dots

My call from Stacey regarding her talk with Briana seemed at first to add nothing more than a big maybe. Joan's reaction to her nanny's death and her radical friends at that time might be a factor, but that was so many years ago it seemed a stretch.

Too much still didn't fit.

I asked if she could find out if Adam knew who along with Jim was there in the "lab."

"I'm meeting him later today. I've been able to sell my story as a radical anti-government type like him. He's promised to try and get me into the back freezer where they keep the bodies. That may be a lot of smoke; I'm not sure he's allowed back there."

I laughed, "And what have you had to promise?"

"Nothing so far. He's actually been quite nice in his weird sort of way. If this really is some major plot, I don't think he understands it. To him it's all a game that allows him to indulge in his fascination with death."

She paused. "I don't want to sleep with the guy, but I am kind of fond of him. Hate to think about it, but if there is a grand plan, he won't be left around as a witness."

"Call me after the visit. They might be planning a follow up to the Boston Marathon. We need to move quickly."

As I hung up, the phone was buzzing. It was my pal, Sergeant Perez.

CHAPTER 38

A New Wrinkle

"Tony, did you speak with your FBI friend in Paris?"

"Yes, she said she had worked with a fellow years ago who now runs the FBI office in Tampa. I've read they had a lot of convictions in Tampa with the cocaine trade. Her friend may know about what's going on here as well."

Perez was quiet for a moment. Knowing her as I do, I was sure an idea was coming. It was a good one.

"Tampa, the FBI was recently in the news there. FBI Director Mueller gave an award to a local attorney, Tammy something, for all her good works including — get this — as vice president of People for Haiti — they raise money for Haitian causes. Just recently she personally raised money to set up a clean water system for an orphanage in Haiti, to prevent cholera."

"Great, Perez. Have you tried to contact her? She may know Joan."

"Left a message, no word back yet. But this is a busy woman. I'd like to know if she has a direct connection to Haiti, like Joan had with her nanny. Or if she knows Joan."

"What about you, Tony, any luck?"

"No, and I'm not sure who else to try, other than Kate. I just her saw a few days ago, and think she'd have called if there was anything new. I'm not sure where to go with this."

"I know Tony. I can't believe it. Everyone I have spoken to officially or not either really knows nothing or shuts up the minute I raise the issue. Particularly any questions about their contact with Joan. They may be watching and waiting for her to slip up, to nail her for something specific."

I realized I was nodding in agreement; I must be losing it.

"Or maybe, Perez, they are hoping she will lead them to whatever group is behind the whole deal."

"Possible. I suspect Emily is your best source. She's high enough up in the bureau to get answers. But what about this guy Joan took to the zombie house or whatever it's called?"

"The brain surgeon. Frank and Elsa have been frequenting the Grill and Table 26, hoping to get a lead on Joan's brain surgeon friend. Seems lately he and Joan are not together as often. I don't have the details, but…"

I stopped mid sentence.

"The brain surgeon. I just remembered Rebecca said she thought he might be originally from Persia, which is now Iran."

"You may have hit on something, Tony. Of course, a lot of people who grew up in Persia left, not pleased with their country being run by the Ayatollah."

"Frank has the guys name. Can you call him and get it, see if anyone has a handle on his background?"

"Will do."

CHAPTER 39

The Pompano Mosque

I headed home and was sorting through some old files that Jimmy left at my condo years ago; maybe there would by a clue as to his connection to Joan.

The cell rang. It was Frank.

"Tony, I spoke with the famous Sonya Perez. She said the brain guy lives in Wellington, attends or used to attend a Shiite mosque in Lauderdale. So I call a friend who I guessed might attend the same mosque. He said yes, he knew of the brain guy, nickname's Ben. His real name is Behrouz, means lucky."

I was thinking of a reply when he continued, "Get this! Ben, Mr. lucky, is not too welcome at that mosque. With 9/11 and all the negative stuff going on, these people just want to be good American citizens. Last thing they want is some radical that taints them all with the 'crazy brush.' My friend, who only knows of him, thought Ben left the country every so often to travel, but he didn't know where."

"What do you think, Frankie. Terrorist training? Joan must know something about his background. Sounds like she's up to her ears in this deal. What could have turned her? The zombie Haiti connection I can see, but from there to Al Qaeda is a big jump. Maybe we can find out what turned her."

Frank replied, "No, first of all this is a Shitte mosque he attended, which would be typical Iran. Not that a terrorist is not a terrorist, but this guy is not Al Qeada, which is Sunni. He's Shiite.

But you're right. Something is sure out of whack. I can't get the image of my pal Ralph at the West Palm Station out of my head. He sure shut up when we asked about the hit and run. His reaction wasn't normal. It wasn't as though he knew nothing, his response wasn't a shrug. He was pushing the whole deal away, and hard.

It has to be someone higher up that he's afraid of crossing, maybe the feds. Our best chance might be Emily in Paris. Wasn't she checking and getting back to you?"

"Yeah, haven't heard yet."

CHAPTER 40

Emily and Gabriella

They had shared a late dinner of boiled lobster in the exquisite wine cellar of the Wald Hotel. Jonas, the manager and a lover of fine wines, knew Emily as a renter of a large suite at the hotel, probably knew she was U.S. government, but had no knowledge of Gabriella, other than as a tourist.

He had invited them to sample the latest shipment of Chassekas, a white wine which is grown throughout Europe, but seems to thrive and produce it's best grapes in the hills near lake Geneva.

They were thanking Jonas and getting set to leave when Emily spotted a text on her cell. She mouthed the words "Palm Beach" to Gabriella, excused herself, and stepped into the outer hall.

It was her friend Pitt from the Tampa office. "Why do you want to know about activities in Palm Beach?"

"Well Pitt, I am from the states you know," drew no reply.

"Seriously, Emily, all I know is we have an undercover person working on a case in Palm Beach. Who it is and the details are only known to a few. I am not privy to specifics. I can only say from the secrecy involved that it could be major."

"No way I can find out more, Pitt? I got a call from an acquaintance that lives in Palm Beach, asking if we were involved. This person knows as much, or possibly more than we do. He will be calling me back and could be of help."

"Sorry, I just know nothing," Pitt replied and hung up.

The two women thank their host again and started back upstairs.

Once in the lobby, Gabriella linked her arm in Emily's. "It's a beautiful night, let's get a little exercise. Walk off that lobster."

They had only traveled half a block when Gabriella asked, "How is your love life? Still running on steroids?"

Emily gave a little girl giggle. "We must have talked for two hours last night. He's coming to Zurich, and told me I could choose the hotel. I've scheduled a four-day stay at the Park Hyatt. It's a beautifully modern hotel right in the center of the city. The reservation clerk was describing the shopping and Opera House in the area, all the hotel amenities. I interrupted and said, 'I just want the biggest king size bed you have. We'll be spending all four days in bed.' He laughed, and replied, 'Excellent, but we are known for our room service, should you eventually get hungry.'"

Gabriella hugged her friend. "I can't tell you how happy I am for you. I only wish..."

"Yes," replied Emily, "you should have the same. What has it been, two years?" then turned, faced her friend, and with her hands on her shoulders. "Go, life is short."

Gabriella, whose feelings of joy for her friend had been interspersed with the hollowness in her own heart, smiled. "Two years is long enough. I will arrange it. Somehow I will see him."

What Gabriella had never mentioned to Emily was, after her enemies had tried to kidnap Tony, she had assigned someone to keep an eye on both him and her father's close friend Emile. Sonja Perez, who had been with Tony as he suffered through his loss of Gabriella, had proved to be a silent ally. Gabriella had indirect contact with Perez though an occasional text message sent from a phone in Palm Beach. Because of this she had been aware of what Tony and Frank were dealing with.

They had strolled a few blocks, looking in shop windows at the latest fashions and breathing in the crisp clear air that Davos is known for, when Gabriella said, "I have a person in the Palm Beach area, perhaps I can help with this problem." She slowed and faced her friend. "Without Anthony's knowing, of course."

"Of course," was the reply.

CHAPTER 41

Spying on Spies

Gabriella had learned from her late father to understand and take advantage of the jealousies and turf battles between individual FBI offices, as well as between the CIA, referred to as the Ivy League, and the FBI, referred to as the "Beer and Brats."

The mistakes and oversights that might have prevented 9/11, like Dick Cheney's fixation on Iraq instead of Bin Laden and the lack of communication between FBI and CIA offices, was fixed in typical government fashion. They invaded Iraq and added more agencies like Homeland Security and the National Counterterrorism Center, all four now vying with each other for higher budgets and more power.

Gabriella, hearing from her Palm Beach source about Tony's involvement in this zombie deal, had decided to take a more practical approach.

She knew Palm Beach wealth attracts its share of fakes, phonies, and hangers-on. She also knew it attracts its share of both men and women who understand, as the song says: "A kiss may be grand but it won't pay the rental."

Many women provide a valuable service to society and expect to be well rewarded for their company. The targets are older wealthy men, married, but wanting someone to keep them feeling young, as well as wealthy New York money managers, too busy to devote time to a real relationship. Many professional service providers, plus in-dependent contractors, have retainers in the $20,000 a month range to be available "when needed."

Gabriella's people had information on several exceptionally at-tractive Brazilian women that, if disclosed, could get them deported in a hurry. They were happy to help.

Two of these women had been assigned to Behrouz, the brain surgeon.

As a result, Joan Diamond, had recently found herself seeing less of Mr. Lucky.

To date, they had not been able to gain access to more than Mr. Lucky's pocketbook for fancy balls and shopping sprees, but were at least able to keep track of his whereabouts.

Others, looking on from afar, were not happy with this arrange-ment at all.

CHAPTER 42

Stacey's Tour

"Tony, I finally got the tour; we had to be fitted with a space suits and masks. Didn't think Adam could get me back there, but he did. He thinks there must be about twenty-five bodies in what they call the vault. We had to look through a large glass petition. I didn't get close enough to the faces to see if your friend Jimmy, was there."

She hesitated for emphasis. "They clearly aren't dead, or really even frozen. We had to go through a series of sealed doors. The air pressure in each new section is lower so air doesn't escape. They are all in space suits with respirators on modest sized beds with sort of like intravenous tubes attached to the suit and into their arms, which gives them food, water, plus whatever drug they use to keep them in this semi-conscious state."

She was quiet for a moment, and then said, "I wonder how they got all this equipment here. There is a lot of stuff."

"Stacey, with all the old folks in this town we have large emergency vehicles up the wazoo, not to mention the supersized Rolls Royce's. But sealed doors so the air doesn't escape? What's that all about?"

"Not sure, Tony, but I know our government has facilities like this with sealed doors and lowered air pressure so no air or germs can escape. They use them for experiments with pandemic type diseases like

Bird Flu, which have the potential to spread like wildfire, and decimate the population in an entire area. Bird Flu is a serious problem in China as we speak. Kills about one out of five who get it, while the rest get real sick with cough, fever, muscle aches, and diarrhea. Once it gets started it's tough to control 'cause it mutates into different strains so fast."

"Wow, you think they plan to infect these people in the vault and then let them out, maybe take them where there are crowds of people, like to a Miami Heat playoff game? Put them in vendor uniforms coughing away and handing out hot dogs and popcorn? Could cause some serious damage.

I'm a Celtics fan, but really."

"Don't kid, Tony. That's a very possible scenario."

"Did you get any idea where they got the bodies?"

"Well, other than Jimmy, seems there are very few from the morgue. Apparently there are a couple of Southern Florida hospitals, or maybe a care center is a better word, that was involved in this Oxycontin scam. When things got hot in that business, they sold out to some overseas group that's supposedly set up as a non-profit. Help the indigent with illness, operations, and so forth, seems occasionally one of these patients with no family connections are, I guess, drugged and shipped here."

"Does Adam know why are they accumulating all these bodies?"

"Adam was told it's for medical experiments, bringing them close to death and then back. That's why he's so excited about it. Thinks he'll get to talk to them afterward. Find out what it's like on the other side."

She took a deep breath. I could almost see her shaking her head. "I don't see the medical experiments bit. There is no operating facility, and according to what he knows, other than a recent group, most of the stiffs — all men by the way — have been there for a while."

"Strange that only Jimmy came from the morgue. That was Joan's lead into this whole operation, other than her friendship with the brain guy. We first got involved with this mess because I read he'd been run over. When we went looking, Joan had spirited his body out of the morgue."

"No, Tony. I found out from Adam that Joan has been involved with the brain guy for some time. He confirmed she had used her Palm Beach connections to get the building, set up the lab, the whole deal. Plus, she's in real estate, would know what property was out of the way and available. I don't know how Jimmy came into play, unless they were using him as a trial to see if they could start pulling bodies from morgues. I also don't really understand Adam's connection, other than he's at the morgue and somehow knows Joan. But this overseas group that bought up these OxyContin labs is definitely in the mix.

Seems like the brain surgeon is running this whole deal."

My cell was beeping. It was Frank. "Thanks, Stacey. I got to take it — it's Frank. I want to try and meet with him and Sonja, see what they can add to the puzzle."

"Great, Tony. Call me when you get anything."

"I will. Nice job, Salome." She giggled at the reference and hung up.

CHAPTER 43

This is it Café

I called Frank, then Sonja, and gave them a brief outline of my conversation with Stacey. Rather than go into detail on cell phones, I suggested we meet at a little place on 24th Street called "This is it Café."

Things were getting to what might be a critical stage. The possibility that with all the people each of us had involved, something might get back to Joan or her partner, "Persia Ben," was increasing exponentially. Not that we're movie stars, but we needed to talk without interruptions, and between us we know a lot of folks that know a lot of folks.

I put the top down to enjoy another beautiful Florida day, flipped on a Sinatra CD and cranked it up. "I've got you under my skin, I've got you deep in the heart of me" was blaring out as I headed across the Flagler Bridge and took a right on Dixie. A little bit of traffic slowed the mile trip, but I didn't care. I had the feeling after talking with Emily that Gabriella and I were going to somehow get together. My mood was up. By the time I turned the corner and headed up 24th, Sinatra had launched into a Cole Porter favorite and I was singing along. "Night and day, you are the one. Only you beneath the moon and under the sun....."

As I pulled into the parking lot, I glanced toward the end of the block. There was the sign: Sunset Bar and Grill. A reminder of the night I was pushed by Frank to dump Nila and Miranda and meet his friend, Vinnie Carangelo.

Oh, well. What's another 35 years?

The best waitress in the area, my friend Jackie, was talking with Frank and Perez in a booth to the right of the door. Jackie is a former Green's Pharmacy waitress who moved to another great spot closer to home. Instead of churchgoers and locals like me, they get the fast growing Northwood area and the boating crowd that loves the eggs and tilapia or salmon cakes, a breakfast favorite available all day.

Jackie gave me a big smile. "I'll get your coffees and then you can order after Tony gets settled. I sat down next to Perez and found myself staring at an uncharacteristically scowling Frank.

Frank leaned toward me and said in a half whisper, "I just got a call from Ralph. He said we should back off."

I leaned toward Frank and said as softly as I could, "Back off from what?"

"That's what I said," replied Frank. "Ralph said, 'You guys are poking around in a situation over there in Palm Beach that is way over your head, and mine. It's being handled.' and he hung up."

Sitting there watching us was a smiling Perez. "Boys, relax. It's nothing personal. Sources I've counted on for information for years won't say a word. Clearly, someone very high up is not only aware of what Joan Diamond and this brain surgeon are doing, but have it under control."

I had just finished filling them in on my conversation with Stacey when Jackie came back with a big smile.

"Cheer up guys and girl. I've never seen this group so serious. It's a beautiful day and the salmon cakes are delicious. Oh, the chef just pulled the turkey out of the oven. The turkey club is incredible."

Frank and I ordered the turkey club, Perez the salmon cakes. Jackie mouthed the word "smile" and left.

I continued. "Do you think the FBI or CIA, whoever handles this stuff, has been communicating with Stacey? She's an ex-spook. Maybe she's told them the same story she told me."

Perez was shaking her head. "She just got involved a short time ago and really because of you two and Elsa."

Frank beamed at the mention of her name. "Elsa is a pretty good reader of people."

"For sure, and has great taste in men," added Sonja, with a big smile.

Frank continued, "Elsa has checked. As best she can tell, both Stacey's background and her sister in West Palm have no holes in their story."

He threw up his hands. "Who else is involved? We have camped out there a number of times. Only Joan Diamond, Lucky Ben, and the Russian that was there when Tony and Stacey went to the door. Oh, and of course Adam and maybe one other low IQ watchman Stacey said seems to have very little idea of what he's watching over."

Perez, who had been doing more listening than talking, finally spoke up. "There is also someone who drove the truck, plus others involved with procuring the bodies, but to the point at hand, fellas, you don't sound too excited about Ralph's call. I think you should be."

"So, Perez, you think the feds know everything that we do and more?" I asked.

"Yes, I do, and I suspect that if they say hands off they mean it. Frank's friend Ralph seems to have known something all along or at least known enough to stay clear of it. What I don't understand is the Diamond woman's role. I know Briana at Main Street News said Joan was radicalized when her nanny died, and she blamed the immigration service, but that was years ago. Seems unlikely she's been working underground all these years."

She shook her head. "On the negative side she did help this guy set up the building, and in some way, somehow, seems to have been closely involved with him all along. They've been at the Grill together, at the building together, and him being disliked at his mosque for his views. Joan must be aware of all this."

Frank winked at me as Perez was going through her usual routine. Logically checking off the factors plus and minus and people involved. That big brain was at work.

I glanced over at Frank. He didn't look convinced that he should back off.

I was on the fence and wondered out loud, "Seems these two spend a lot of time at the Grill. I wonder if Rebecca would have noticed if anyone different seemed to be there observing them."

We were quiet for a bit as Jackie brought our meals. Then Perez said, "You boys have a little more freedom in these areas than I do. I'm taking Ralph's advice and backing off. If I can be of help on the side, great, but I am officially off the case."

Frank, as usual, when the portions are equal, finished first. He stood and did his usual stretch. "Tony, why don't we take a ride over, meet at Bice, and check out the Vault."

Perez held up a hand. "Slow down boys. How much do you know about this Mr. Brain surgeon?" She took a slip of paper from her purse and laid it on the table. It was an address in Wellington followed by two women's names.

"What's that?" said Frank.

"Mr. Lucky's address and names of his two lady friends."

Sergeant Sonya Perez, star detective on the Palm Beach police force, stood and walked slowly toward the door. Once opened, she turned to give us her best smile.

"You men can't see the forest for the trees. If you won't back off, you might as well jump in all the way."

She left, chuckling to herself on the way to her car.

I stood there staring, first at the paper, then at Frank.

CHAPTER 44

Wellington Horse Country

"Argyle Road, never heard of it," said Frank. "Let's take my car. I've got the GPS."

My car has the GPS as well, but I kept still. Frank likes to be in charge. I started working for him as a young guy just of out college. In his mind I'm the same young guy; still wet behind the ears. I love the guy, so I go along.

I punched in the address. "Looks like it's right in the middle of horse country. Go west on Southern about 10 miles, then left on Forest Hills. It's a dead end off Paddock before you get to the polo fields."

Frank was unusually quiet. I could tell something was bothering him. "What's Elsa up to today?" I said, trying to get something going.

"Working, I guess. I didn't see her at all yesterday."

Guessing a lot of this CIA stuff was bringing back memories of the mystery surrounding her husband's death. I tried again. "Everything alright with you two?"

"Yes, things are fine. It's not that. I was just wondering who gave Perez this guy's address, plus names of his girlfriends. Are we being set up?"

"You mean by Perez? No way. We knew he was in Wellington, no problem for her to get the address, unlisted or not. Getting the lowdown on the girlfriends is a little tougher, but not, pardon the pun, brain surgery."

We had located the street. Frank stopped fifty feet beyond the corner and got out.

"Looks like only one big house at the very end. Let's walk down and take a look."

Not sure what Frank had in mind, I followed. The street was unpaved and curved gradually to the left so you could only see the right front corner of the large brick structure about fifty yards away. There were trees and thick bushes along either side, followed by open fields. By walking down the left side we might be unseen by anyone in the house until we were close enough to get a decent look at the place.

He stopped at the point in the curve beyond which we could be seen from the house, but where we could observe through the bushes. I noticed a horse barn and small cottage, probably for the help.

Frank stopped and sat on a low wall, which ran along what was supposed to be the sidewalk.

"What's next, Frankie?"

"Let's just sit a minute. If this guy is planning what we think, he's got to be cautious enough to have cameras set up, may already have spotted us. Plus, he ain't acting alone."

We sat for what seemed to be forever, actually maybe a half-hour, when suddenly two Lincoln MKZ's came tearing down the road. One raced by and parked in front of the house. The second stopped behind us, blocking any chance to leave other than across the open field where we'd have made a couple of easy targets if that was their objective.

A very large gentleman dressed in black opened the driver side door and stepped out. He was holding, but not pointing, a 9mm Glock semiautomatic.

"May I ask you gentlemen what you are doing here?"

Frank spoke first. "Yes, sir, we saw there was a property for sale in this neighborhood and were looking around to see what the area was like."

Still not actually pointing the gun, although he was built like he didn't need it, he said, "I'd suggest you go back and focus on the house that's for sale. This property is off limits."

The accent seemed to be more New York than Florida, but it didn't appear an appropriate time to have that discussion.

We walked swiftly back to the car.

"Tony, did you notice the plates?"

"Yeah, U.S. government, you think FBI?"

He started the car and stepped on the gas. "What I think is someone used Perez to set us up. We need to get out of here in a hurry."

CHAPTER 45

A Night in the Can

Thinking we had been set up, Frank was barreling down Paddock, which swings in a big semi-circle through horse country. He muttered something under his breath that sounded like "The local police may have been called and are coming to cut us off."

We clearly needed a side road to pull off, and there weren't any.

It wasn't clear then or now whether the local police had been tipped off and stopped us to: 1) get us out of the FBI's hair, or 2) 70 miles an hour in a 25 zone caught their interest, or 3) Frank's license plate being somehow missing, or 4) an anonymous complaint that two men in a stolen Cadillac were trying to break into a home on Argyle.

Whatever it was, the local Johns were polite but firm. We were there for the night. Sans cells, except the one we were in.

In these "modern" times, we are so used to having our cell phones to communicate, gain information, and just kill time, I began to realize being without it creates an anxiety similar to a child having their blankie taken away.

When I say we, it doesn't include Frank, who doesn't turn his on half the time anyway so, in spite of the thin mattress on a steel bed, he was sound asleep.

Meanwhile, I was sitting in the semi-darkness trying to sort out what may or may not be happening to us. How did our night in jail relate to the semi-conscious bodies in a supposedly deserted, cement structure in the heart of Palm Beach, and yeah, what was the connection between all this and Joan Diamond and Mr. Lucky?

By the time the lights finally went on, I was focused on the issue of who told Perez to give us that address.

After blinking to adjust my eyes to the bright light, I recognized a grinning Sergeant Sonja Perez on the good side of our steel cage sleeping quarters.

The officer on duty clearly knew Perez and seemed to be deferring to her as to what to do with us, which I hoped was to be our release.

I woke Frank, who sat up slowly and stretched, then stood and stretched again.

Then, while rubbing his eyes as though trying to get his bearings, he finally spotted Perez.

He started to smile, and then remembering how we got here, it turned to a frown. "Was this a set up or what, Perez? Who gave you the address of lucky Ben?"

"Let's sit in the chief's office, and I'll explain what I know."

Sonja led us to the chief's office while the sergeant on duty heated the coffee. She sat behind the big desk; Frank and I sat on one of the two tan, well-worn leather couches.

I glanced around the cluttered room. Off to our right it opened up to a conference table stacked with files and surrounded by ten chairs and a computer screen at the far end. The walls were covered with action photos of galloping polo ponies. Most were signed, mainly best wishes comments in Spanish. Keeping on the good side of the law is apparently smart in any language.

The desk was clear except for a standing photo of what appeared to be his four grandchildren. I was sorry the chief wasn't there. If Frank had been able to pull out his photos and explained his philosophy, "If I had known how much fun it is being a grandfather, I'd have gotten old sooner," he and Frank would definitely connect.

But he wasn't, and the clock on the chief's wall said 4 a.m.

"Well, boys, let me fill you in on the details," she paused, "as I understand them. First, regarding the brain surgeon's address, I remember

Tony saying Rebecca thought he lived in Wellington. What I was going to tell you two before you got your panties in a bunch over Ralph's advice to back off, was a friend at the registry got me the address, and I was curious to check it out myself. Problem is, I'd already gotten more involved than I should have without telling my superiors. When it looked like you weren't going to take Ralph's advice, I didn't have a choice.

I knew you'd go out there, but expected to hear from you afterward. No way I could know the FBI was there.

When I didn't hear, I took a chance and called Ralph. He was so worried about even talking by phone, we met at his apartment at Marina Grande. Beautiful layout, by the way. At any rate, he was very cautious, but reading between the lines it appears the bureau has been watching this guy and Joan Diamond for some time. They were ready to pounce if the brain guy, or whoever he's taking orders from, decided to start their game of infecting the guys in the vault with Bird Flu or some other crazy disease, and sending them out to spread it."

She nodded to herself. "Great plan actually. Who'd expect this in Palm Beach."

"By the time I left Ralph's it was late, but I thought you'd want to know. I called you both and got no answer, so I stopped by Tony's place," she was shaking her head, "which is never locked. Finding no Tony, I guessed it was trouble in Wellington."

I asked, "If they knew all this, why didn't they stop it, close it down?"

"Good question. First of all, the fact that you were picked up on his street means they probably have taken him in, but it seems the reason they delayed was they know of other cells like this in other parts of the country, but they aren't one-hundred percent sure they have them all. Apparently they had a tap on Ben's phones, computers, the works, and getting close to finding where these other zombie houses were. Then, the brain guy got distracted by a couple of Brazilian professionals. Apparently these two were not only very good looking but quite experienced in the sexual arts."

She was giggling to herself. "They were giving him the equivalent of his 72 virgins without having to blow himself up.

This distraction seems to have caused a little extra nervousness for the FBI, and got them to move early. They're not sure of the motive of the Brazilian women beyond the usual sex for sale, but with them in the picture he wasn't following the same daily routine as before. They got concerned he might set things in motion sooner, and boys," she hesitated to give it full impact, "Ralph was very cautious, but with a few nods or head shakes, my guess is the mysterious Joan Diamond has been taken into custody by the FBI as a co-conspirator."

Frank was nodding. "Now I'm even more confused." He held up his index finger as though counting. "First she ran over Jimmy for his insurance; next she picks up the body from the morgue; then she puts him in cold storage, but he's still alive. Now we aren't sure if he's even in there. And what was his deal? Was his death faked to collect on the insurance, or was he drugged so he appeared dead? And is he now one of these guys in a zombie state that is going to be diseased and released to cause havoc?"

He stopped as though visualizing Jim. "With his nine lives luck, he's probably left the country and is on a tropical island somewhere with a couple of bikini clad girlfriends."

Unsure of how many points he had covered, he stopped to see how many fingers he had up, grinned, closed his fist, and continued.

"And Joan, remember, conveniently got her so-called fiancé, who owned land with Nila's father, to die. We don't know if she helped or not, but it sure seems to have worked to her advantage. Then she used her State House connections to get the inside scoop on the land they owned and neglected to tell Nila the real value. Probably not illegal, but really.

Then she hangs out with the brain surgeon who seems to be running this scheme. Actually she doesn't just hang out, apparently helps him find the building and set up the whole operation. Was she just selling real estate? I don't think so. She knew what was going on in the building; she helped get the permits and knew it held the bodies. Tony saw her leaving."

Watching Frank again try to count on his fingers to make points, and then deciding if things like "legal, by the way" meant he should drop from four fingers to three, had gotten his thought process a little muddled.

Even I was getting confused "Are you trying to judge if she's guilty or not? She had that incident with her nanny being killed in an accident because the feds made a mistake. That was a long time ago, but whoever is running this zombie scam may have known about it and reminded her. Or maybe she's like Adam and only knows part of what's going down."

Sonja was shaking her head. "From where I stand, she's up to her neck in this deal. My guess is the FBI has her dead to rights. She's been involved with the brain guy on some basis since he arrived in town. As Frank just said, she helped him get the building, get the permits, and I just don't understand the angle with Jim — unless that was to distract anyone that might be watching," she smiled and pointed, "like you two."

She stood and gave a stretch that would have made Frank proud. "I've got to get some sleep. No need for me to stick around. Just wanted to be sure my two favorite sleuths were OK and tell you what I know, or think I know.

As soon as the chief gets in, you guys will be heading back to Palm Beach. Call me tomorrow."

She picked her car keys up off the desk and started to leave just as the sergeant stepped into the room. "Sorry folks. I spoke with the chief. He's on his way over. Detective Perez is free to go, but you two are staying until the chief gets here and can clear your release with the FBI."

Almost in unison, Frank and I said, "What?"

"Not my rules boys. You can sit here and wait quietly or I can put you back in the cell."

I looked straight at him. "What has the FBI got to do with us?"

"Seems someone got in the middle of the investigation and they want to know if you have any ideas as to who it might be. Beyond that is above my pay grade."

He walked over and flicked on the TV.

"Make yourselves comfortable. The chief will be here soon."

CHAPTER 46

The Wait

After questioning the sergeant multiple times as to why we were being held, Perez had finally realized he was just taking orders and left.

We settled in to wait, and wait.

Finally, at about ten-thirty, the chief, who either had a lot of other more important business or for some reason was stalling, arrived to find me on his couch watching a re-run of Woody Allen's Midnight in Paris.

I happen to love the movie, and though I'd seen it in total once and in pieces several times, I was a little disappointed that he would arrive just when Woody's character is listening to Cole Porter on the piano singing "Let's Fall in Love," while chatting with Scott and Zelda Fitzgerald.

Turns out I had no reason to worry about missing the scene. The chief stuck his head in the door and announced, "I'll be with you in a moment fellas," and was gone.

Frank was a little less patient. "Son of a bitch locked us up, gave us no opportunity to call a lawyer. My constitutional rights have been invaded," he shouted after the chief.

Hoping to shut him up in the middle of my favorite scene, I said, "Frankie, relax. We never asked to make a call to a lawyer, and someone did tell Perez we were here."

"We didn't ask because we weren't charged with anything. What's the stall for?"

Actually, I was thinking the same thing. It did seem the chief had been here for what was now over an hour, but I needed to calm Frank down. "Once the word gets out on this guy's being arrested, the chief is going to have to deal with the press, along with the town's people who are nervous, as well as the just plain curious. He may be dealing with this stuff now."

Frank was alternating between sitting and pacing. Perez had promised Frank she would contact Elsa, and it was hours since she had left. Elsa had neither shown up nor tried to make contact. I suspected he was more concerned about Elsa than where the chief might be.

My early questions as to whether she was somehow involved had been resolved some time ago, but Frank's pacing brought them back.

But no, I thought, she hated the CIA over the loss of her husband, but not the country. Plus, this seemed to be FBI.

But why hadn't she shown up or made contact?

Around noon, the chief finally arrived, shook hands and moved toward his desk. "Sorry, fellas. We don't discover terrorist groups living in our midst that often. I've been rather busy."

Frank, now standing and towering over the chief, said, "We understand chief, but please explain what that has to do with us?"

CHAPTER 47

Maguire and Gildea

The chief pointed to the door as two very handsome young men in dark blue suits, white shirts, blue and white stripped ties, and black square-toed shoes entered the room.

"Gentlemen, I'd like to introduce agents Connor Maguire and Sean Gildea. They would like to ask a few questions regarding your involvement in this case."

I nodded to Frank and said, "Guess this is why they were delaying, waiting for these two to arrive."

The chief walked to the door the two men had entered. "Call if you need me," left and closed the door behind him.

Maguire's hair seemed a little long to be a button-down FBI type. It was sandy with a tinge of color that made me think he was probably a red head as a kid. Pure Irish on both sides I guessed. Had to have a good-looking mother. He pointed toward the conference table. "Why don't we sit in there, where we can talk, and agent Gildea can take a few notes."

Agent Gildea took out his notepad and smiled. "Are you familiar with the name Ramadon Abdullah Mohammad Shallah?"

Before either of us could give him an obvious no, he continued, "This guy has a PhD in banking and economics, which he has used in interesting ways — like money laundering, racketeering, murder, and bombings. He's a founder and head guy of the Palestinian Islamic

Jihad, which, until recent problems in Syria, was headquartered in Damascus."

I was nodding, but not sure where he was heading until he said, "This guy is your brain surgeon, Behrouz Rabbani's boss. They are our very deadly non Al-Qeada- Iran type enemies."

He stopped to emphasize the point.

"Up until this situation, we had assumed the new Shiite tactic was to attack us by turning our basic freedom of the press against us. You know, publish Internet articles on how to make bombs, articles preaching that killing infidels is the word of Allah, that type of garbage."

Gildea, who looked like he was working hard to show a serious FBI face but could break into a devilish grin at any time, was shaking his head for emphasis. "The scope of this operation in Palm Beach was a real shocker. The Shia's tend to be less dramatic. This tactic of creating homegrown terrorists like the Boston Marathon brothers seemed to be their main thrust."

He hesitated for emphasis. "This had the potential to be a 9/11 type event."

Conner broke in and said, "We have a pretty good handle on who you two have been involved with, and understand you probably didn't realize the seriousness of this business until very recently."

I turned to Frank, "Yeah, we were going through the steps of moving from Joan Diamond killing our friend for his insurance, to using these people as guinea pigs for the brain surgeon to test drugs, or turn into zombies for who knows what purpose."

Frank, still annoyed at being unable to reach Elsa, cut me off. "Is it true that Joan Diamond has been taken into custody?"

"We can't comment on that sir," was Sean's quick and very official sounding reply."

"What about Elsa Larsen?" I asked.

The two agents exchanged a slightly puzzled look, then agent Gildea replied, "We can't comment on that sir."

I had hoped their slight delay was enough to make Frank comfortable that she wasn't arrested or involved.

No such luck. He pushed his chair back from the table and stood, hands on hips.

"Is there something specific you fellows are fishing for? Because I'm tired and have more important things to do than dance with you two."

Connor frowned. "We understand, sir. There is just one issue, and then we'll get out of your hair. Somehow this Behrouz Rabbani fellow got, shall we say, distracted, by two Brazilian women who normally come at a pretty good tariff. We're trying to figure out if they got involved by chance, or whether someone else was pulling the strings."

He paused and smiled. "I have never been to Brazil, but if these two are any indication of what the women are like, it's my next vacation."

Sean interrupted. "We also know that Iran is setting up sleeper cells in Brazil and several other South American countries. We are interrogating these two women to see if there is any connection."

"Like what? That they were recruited and working for Iran or a Brazilian group against Iran," asked Frank.

"We don't know, but it seems someone was covering their cost and may have recruited them to keep an eye on Behrouz. We just need to find a connection. You two have been doing a lot of poking around. Any ideas?"

I looked at Frank and shrugged. He was shaking his head.

Maguire stood up and held out his hand. "Thanks for taking the time gentlemen, and please, you two live here. People are more apt to open up to you than two 'suits' from the FBI. Anything you can pick would be gratefully appreciated. Here's my card."

CHAPTER 48

Home at Last

The missing plate on Frank's Caddie, one of the reasons we had been held, was miraculously back on the car. They had obviously given the car the once over.

Everything was back to normal, even Frank, who, while heading east on Southern, had finally reached Elsa. I could tell by his "dancing with sugar plums" Christmas smile that all was well.

She had relatives show up unexpectedly and was planning to meet him after work at her place.

As for me, I had not managed to sleep on that thin mattress on the steel slab in a hot cell, and I was just plain tired.

Frank dropped me at my car, at the This is it Café.

I headed back across the Flagler Bridge and home.

I shut off my cell phone and the house phone, closed the drapes, locked the doors and crashed.

CHAPTER 49

A Surprise

I woke late. It was after nine.

Moving slowly, I got up, hopped into my favorite Gardeur everyday pants, a tee shirt, and unlaced sneakers, and made my usual walk to Green's.

There were probably messages on my cell phone, but I decided to ignore life for a bit and relax.

The fine young men of the FBI had the case all wrapped up.

Later, I would call Perez and take a ride by the vault to see how they brought Jimmy and the so called zombie's back to normal, and maybe find out what had happened to Adam.

But for now, coffee and eggs Benedict at Greens was first on the list.

I passed my friend Dr. Rose coming out of Greens for his daily constitutional. He gave a big smile and a "Hello, Tony" as he passed.

Dorothy, an archaeologist, when not waitressing, was telling Nancy about a talk she had given on the history of the island before white settlers arrived. There's a current fight over who has the right to artifacts on private property.

Beyond my current mental pay grade I thought and grabbed a seat alone at the end of the bar.

Patty brought me my large half de-caf and half regular with milk and pointed to the eggs Benedict on the blackboard.

I nodded, took a sip of my coffee, and decided to pick up the paper while I waited for the eggs.

I grabbed the Palm Beach Post, and there, sure enough, was the front page: FBI Uncovers Zombie House in Palm Beach, with a story about drugged men that were captured and held by a foreign power, possibly Iran.

The subheading was not what I expected.

In bold print was: UNDERCOVER FBI AGENT, JOAN DIAMOND, CRACKS MAJOR CASE.

The AP article headlined every paper on the shelf from the Shiny Sheet to the New York Times. The article went on to say that Diamond was first recognized by the Division of Homeland Security and later by the FBI for her diligent efforts as a uniformed watchman after 9/11. Her sharp observations and key insight into people was quickly recognized. After recruiting her to provide short term, as needed, undercover services, she was asked to infiltrate this Iranian plot. Details are top secret, but this writer believes an FBI mole in the Palestinian Islamic Jihad (PIJ) recommended her as a contact for their Palm Beach operation by showing old photos of her and members of the Freedom from Oppression Party (FOP) who tried to blow up the federal building in Tallahassee years before.

Behrouz Rabbani, arrested as the mastermind of the operation, contacted her posing as a potential real estate buyer, struck up a friendship and recruited her to his cause. She, of course, was more than willing to oblige. In his mind he was recruiting a local person as a potential terrorist, when in fact she was working undercover for the FBI.

Also arrested were the operators and workers in each of three former Oxycodone clinics that had been shut down, but then reopened by this same foreign group under the guise of recovery clinics. Those addicts unfortunate enough to have no known relatives were put in this zombie state and sent to the Palm Beach lab.

The operation had been in full swing for over three years, with Joan even going so far as to appear to run over a local man for his insurance and then remove him from the morgue to their lab.

Without Rabbani's knowledge, she later arranged for him to be released and flown out of the country.

An unidentified person with the West Palm Beach police created files on her prior anti-government activities to bolster her story and protect her real identity.

I reached for my coffee and took a sip. It was ice cold, as were my eggs Benedict.

Nancy was standing there, hands on hips, smiling.

"See you enjoyed the eggs, Tony. Probably want seconds?"

I love exchanging barbs with Nancy, but was too much in shock. (Plus, she usually wins.)

I smiled, picked up the paper, and headed to the front counter, got the Journal and the New York Times and headed back to the condo.

No wonder there were all those messages on my cell.

CHAPTER 50

Messages from Friends, Plus One

Sure enough, my iPhone must have shown a dozen messages on the glass, the first one from Frank. "Tony, did you see the headlines? Joan Diamond was with the FBI all along, sure had me fooled. Those two agents that sprung us from jail were great at keeping secrets."

Then Perez, "Tony, call me. Now that this zombie caper is settled, we need a new excuse to hook you up with Emily." She was laughing. "So Emily can re-hook you up with Gabriella."

I smiled. My good, sweet pal Perez. Always gets to the heart of the issue — no pun intended.

Then Stacey, "Great ending to what might have been a sorry tale. Stop by Main Street News to say hello. Maybe we can get Briana to invite us to dinner, sample her great Italian cooking."

Finally a number I didn't recognize. "Connor Maguire sir, just reminding you that we could use any tips on where these two Brazilian hotties came from."

I smiled at the thought. Wonder if his interest in connecting them was strictly FBI.

The CD I had turned on earlier was playing Louie Armstrong and Ella Fitzgerald singing, "Birds do it, bees do it, even educated fleas do it. Let's do it. Let's fall in love."

Everyone and everything but me, it seemed.

I stretched out on the couch and started going through the many articles on the illustrious Joan Diamond.

I was looking for anything new. Not much there, most of it was her family background, past and present. I was interested to read she has a number of grandchildren, which seemed unusual considering how young she looks.

Articles were mostly stuff they could dig up from old papers; the FBI had clearly given out very little. There was no mention of the Brazilian women that agent Maguire had asked about, or Jimmy's car accident.

I was on my third paper and nodding off. Ella and Louie were now on Gershwin. Ella was singing, "The way you wear your hat, the way you sip your tea, the memory of all that…"

Just the word memory jogged mine. Thoughts of Gabriella flooded back. Sitting on her couch while she showed me pictures of her childhood as a way to explain who she was, and the life she was locked into by a family that was now gone. Visions of making love.

I jumped up and flicked off the CD. Too many memories only emphasized what I had and may not have again.

I noticed there had been another, more recent, call on my cell.

It was Frank again; "Elsa and I would like to invite you to a late brunch at her apartment. Anytime, probably eat about one-thirty or two. Sonja and Stacey are coming. We can talk about this case we solved," he was laughing, "or almost screwed up."

I checked my watch. It was ten minutes to one.

Still a little groggy from trying to sleep off the hectic events of the last few days, and needing a diversion from the thoughts of Gabriella, which drifted in and out, I walked to the beach and stood staring out to sea, half in the moment and half in a future that may never come.

On the way back, I passed the lobby of my building and realized I hadn't been to pick up my mail in a couple days. This is normal. I avoid my mailbox that's usually stuffed with invitations to three hundred dollar and up fundraisers at The Breakers or Mar-A-Lago, where Donald Trump struts in at the head of the procession as though he's putting on the party for free.

He ain't!

I attended an affair with my friend who raised millions over the years for local kids, and asked how much of my $325 she got. "All goes to Donald" was the reply.

Along with the fundraiser invites are a dozen others from every hospital or museum you've ever visited, plus all the political stuff. Lots of very worthy causes that seem to assume because you live in Palm Beach, you must be rich.

Wish I were and could give more.

I had pulled the mail out of my box and sat down at the center table to sort through the dozen plus pieces.

Two politicals asking for my opinion, but really just wanting money. Trash. Couple of renewals for magazines I never read. Trash. Three more solicitations and two invitations to balls and fundraisers. Trash.

I was stuffing everything but an insurance form in the trash when Bonnie, our favorite mail lady, was just getting out of her truck.

I held the door as she came through with her sack of mail for the building.

"You look happy today. What did you do win the sweepstakes, Bonnie?

"No, nothing like that, but we went to the casino last night. I don't bet much, but I won what was a nice pot for me."

"Good for you, Bonnie. Maybe you can bring me some luck in the form of something other than groups asking me for money."

She reached in her sack and pulled out a couple pieces with my name on them. "Here you go, Tony, even one that looks personal. Don't get many of those anymore."

I took it from her and smiled. "I remember these. I think it's called a letter, like we used to get in the old days before email."

She went about her business of sorting the mail in the boxes as I turned the plain white envelope over.

No return address, but my name and address was handwritten in a large scrawl. Pleasantly curious, I studied it for a few seconds, and then tore it open. The handwriting seemed familiar, but I wasn't sure who it could be.

Inside was a photo of two attractive women in very revealing bikinis with palm trees and the green-blue ocean surf behind them.

I stared for a minute in disbelief.

In the center was a guy with a big "cat that ate the canary" smile.

It was Jimmy.

I turned the photo over and there on the back was a poem:

> *Perhaps you thought that I was free,*
> *From life on earth for eternity.*
> *But instead of that place where they do the burnin,*
> *I'm here on the beach satisfying my yearnin.*

It was postmarked three days earlier from the Dominican Republic.

Was this a joke, an old photo someone had found and thrown into an envelope to blow my mind?

No way. The poem was pure Jimmy.

And no coincidence that the Dominican Republic and Joan's Haiti are two countries on the same Caribbean Island. Had someone traveled a few hours by bus to mail a letter on the other side of the border in the Dominican?

Back in my condo I pulled out a file of poems and rhymes written by Jim.

The top sheet in the folder, written in longhand was:

> *A healthy heart*
> *I understand that nuts and fruit*
> *Are best to eat in one's pursuit*
> *Of sustaining a strong and healthy heart*
> *But eating that stuff can make one fart*
> *So the answer that I pursue my dear*

Is, if at times when I am near
And feel that rumbling in my rear
With no excuse, no time for ruse
I leave the room to let one loose
Would you calmly act like nothing occurred?
Continue our discussion without skipping a word
Or make a fuss and try and pretend
That I'm hardly even a casual friend
Insist I immediately take you home
And force me to live to one hundred alone?

Same handwriting. Same crazy guy. I sat for a moment and re-read Jimmy's poem, flipped it over and stared again at the photo. The guy had one crazy co-dependent relationship after another, finally hit the skids after a bad one, then has his death faked by Joan, who probably got him sober, and he ends up on a beach with two gorgeous women.

Talk about nine lives.

Then I thought about the state of my world.

Frank was happy and healthy with a great woman. Sonja helped us out as best she could and kept her nose clean. We gained a new friend in Stacey.

I should be happy, and guess I was, but Auntie Sonja, as usual, read me right.

There was a big hole in my heart I had hoped connecting with Emily would solve. But I no longer had an excuse to reconnect with Emily and as Perez said, by default with Gabriella.

I went into the bedroom to change, still wondering, daydreaming about a lost love.

Emily's too busy running an important office in Paris, I thought, to locate Gabriella and reconnect us. It's not like she and Gabriella are pals.

Enough! Get dressed and join your friends.

CHAPTER 51

The Surprise of the Ages

The blue blazer I had worn at Harriet's funeral a week ago was still draped over a chair. One week isn't close to a record, by the way.

I picked it up, then realizing the lunch at Elsa's would be casual, and I checked the pockets before I hung it in the closet.

There, scribbled in large print was Sergeant Perez 561-832- ---- .

It took a few seconds to register. The bold print, the last time I wore the jacket was the funeral, Emile!

This was the number he handed me at the Sail Fish Club when I had asked about Joan and he had asked about Gabriella.

What could it possibly mean? Sonja had information on Joan? On Gabriella?

Perez would be there. I finished dressing and headed to the car.

The Slade is across the bridge and a little north, just past the hospitals. It's a very well run complex of two attached buildings with great views of the lake and the Palm Beach shoreline with its row of super mansions and yachts. From the upper floors you can see Palm Beach, The Breakers, and beyond to the Atlantic. In many ways the view is better than the one in Palm Beach, which looks back at West Palm. Plus, I might add, the view is not just better, but a couple of decimal points cheaper.

I pulled into the valet stand and headed through the attractive lobby decorated with variations of beautiful blown glass.

Elsa's place is on the fourteenth floor — a three bedroom with direct water views.

I started to knock, but noticing the door was open, I stepped into the entryway.

The kitchen was to my right, and straight ahead was the dining room/living room area where a table was set up with assorted sandwich halves, dips, several salads, quiche, and a roasted chicken. Beyond the spacious living room was the deck and view of Palm Beach.

Elsa came in from the deck where they were all sitting and gave me a big hug. "All's well that ends well. Please let me help you with the buffet." She handed me a plate and pointed to her quiche: "This is Frank's favorite, so I made extra."

I smiled. It seems Frank is over the early stages of romance and found his real appetite again.

The large deck allowed the five of us to sit comfortably around three sides of a rectangular table and enjoy the view. They were involved in a discussion of who did what to whom, including Adam, who apparently was intensely interviewed by agents Maguire and Gildea, then released when Joan vouched for him as not knowing what was really going down.

The seat next to Perez closest to the door was open. She gave me a wink and whispered, "Glad you are alright, Tony. It was kept out of the papers, but it seems Frank's pal Ralph at the West Palm P.D. is an old friend of Joan's from years ago, when she and her husband lived in New Haven. He was her local contact and FBI go-between all along."

Still whispering while the main group's conversation continued, "I spoke with Ralph this morning. He said, 'You can't believe the shock I felt when Frank came to visit the day after Patterson's body was discovered, and he arrives with his friend Tony, a private dick of all things.' He said they had pressured the Palm Beach Post to keep the hit and run out of the headlines. Problem was, without telling the Post what was really involved, they had to compromise. They put the story in the obituary where they figured no one would notice."

I was smiling at the memory. "It was Frank's fault." I went on to describe our lunch, Frank's 'Grease Beast, and how Lisa, seeing the difference in size of our orders, handed me the Post knowing I'd probably finish sooner.

"Without the help of the Grease Beast and Frank's appetite, we'd have never known Jimmy was dead."

She laughed. "I can picture the scene. That boy can eat."

I leaned closer and whispered, "I got a letter this morning, post marked Dominican Republic, from guess who?"

"Who?"

"Jimmy. Just a photo of him on the beach with two women in bikinis, had a poem on the back. It was pure Jimmy."

She was shaking her head and smiling. "Nine lives for sure, but so nice he's OK."

Along with enjoying the view, hashing over all that had happened, plus picking at the buffet, over two hours had passed.

I had brought up Emile's note by asking, "You, of course, know Emile DuPont. Any reason he would have suggested I call you regarding Joan or Gabriella?"

She had shrugged and given me her "I have no idea look," then asked if I had contacted Emily and had she mentioned Gabriella?

The answer was no.

We thanked Elsa, said our goodbyes, and while riding down on the elevator together I asked, "Joan's all over the front pages. Did Ralph mention where she is now?"

"Yes, she's off to a wedding in Michigan. She's a bridesmaid in the wedding of an old friend."

I smiled and thought I must one day thank Joan for her creativity.

Then I wondered. I met Eva at the Grill before I followed Joan and discovered the lab. She must have known all along that we were asking about her, checking up on her, and decided to have her friend Eva connect and distract me.

As my car came, Perez squeezed my hand. "Smile buddy, you two will get together a lot sooner than you think."

As I pulled into my parking space, I was thinking about Gabriella.

She had said we would meet again, but that was so open-ended. Would we ever? I should call Emily and ask for her help, her advice. At least if I knew it was over I could move on. There were lots of nice women I was close to, but Gabriella had always been the one.

Still lost in my thoughts and my daydreams of what was possible and what was real, I parked and headed in.

As I opened my door, I heard a voice in the living room behind me. "Anthony."

I recognized the slight Italian accent and turned to see the Gabriella of my dreams, of so many memories, the Gabriella I thought I had lost, rushing into my arms, kissing my lips, my cheeks my neck.

All the passion of that short but intense period two years before came rushing back. With her legs wrapped around my waist, her tongue seeking mine, I carried her in and placed her on my bed.

You're not supposed to look a gift horse in the mouth, but I had to ask.

She smiled. "You have a very special friend in Sonja, and I in Emily, who tricked me into coming to Paris to meet her lover, then drove me to De Gaulle and handed me a ticket."

She kissed me softly on the lips and grinned. "My ticket was one way."

CHAPTER 52

Of Love and Lust

I could go into detail as to what happened next, but as I lay in bed with Gabriella in my arms, I remembered Frank's sermon on lust versus love.

"When it's lust, men tell you all the specifics, all the details.

When men are in love, they talk constantly about the woman and all her charms, but omit the romantic details."

CHAPTER 53

Reality Returns

I had fallen into a long, deep, dreamless sleep that was finally interrupted by the phone ringing in the living room, which I ignored.

But someone was persistent. It rang, stopped, and then rang again. By perhaps the fourth time, I was finally forced to crawl out of bed and answer.

It was Perez. "Tony, there's been an accident. An Air France flight from Paris to the states crashed. Possibly some deaths. We're awaiting details."

I remembered Perez last words when we left together yesterday. "Smile buddy, you two will get together a lot sooner than you think."

Then I thought, why is she telling me this? Gabriella, was she on that flight? No, she was here last night, waiting when I came home. We made love; she fell asleep in my arms.

Was it a dream, my imagination? Is she dead, her spirit came to say goodbye?

I waited for Sonja to continue, to explain.
She was silent.

Made in the USA
Lexington, KY
24 January 2014